I0456797

INTELLIGENT
DESIGN
REVELATIONS

J. M. Erickson

Intelligent Design: Revelations

Senior Editor: Suzanne M. Owen

Cover design: Cathy Helms
Avalon Graphics, LLC
http://www.avalongraphics.org

Layout and eBook conversion done by eB Format
http://www.ebformat.com

Publisher: J. M. Erickson
Blog - https://www.jmeindieblog.com
Publisher website - http://www.jmericksonindiewriter.net

ISBN (MOBI Format): 978-1-942708-39-1
ISBN (ePub Format): 978-1-942708-40-7
ISBN (Softcover): 978-1-942708-41-4

Printed in the United States of America

Praise for *Intelligent Design: Revelations*

"Intelligent, complex, riveting, and with surprising twists, *Intelligent Design: Revelations* was an unexpected treat for me... The technology and advancements were believable and yet almost feel ahead of its time." – ***Indie Book Reviewers***

"Well-written and suspenseful, Erickson's story blends scientific theory with fast-paced action in an adventure that should have its fans practically sitting up and begging for a sequel." – ***US Review of Books***

*"Intelligent Design: Revelations i*s a wonderfully absorbing science fiction novella presenting existential questions that occupy the reader's mind long after the book has been put down." – ***Suzanne M. Owen, Senior Editor***

"The book combines intriguing past and current scientific events and theories, conspiracy, high-tech gadgets and a touch of humor, with a cast of unique characters to give you a gratifying reading experience. It is an interesting read and fans of science fiction will love it" – ***Readers' Favorite***

"...it is to Erickson's credit that he fulfills the absolute criteria for a proper science fiction novel: i.e. science made into fiction—and that should be very enjoyable to sci-fi purists seeking out this exact kind of work." – ***Self-Publishing Review***

"A great read for the true science-fiction lover." – ***Feathered Quilled Book Reviews***

"*Intelligent Design* gives the reader both current and past scientific theories and events, and brings them together in an enticing soup of conspiracy, humour, high-tech gadgets, and existential questions." – ***AIA Reviews***

Other Works by J. M. Erickson

Action/Adventure Thrillers

Albatross: Birds of Flight—Book One
Raven: Birds of Flight—Book Two
Eagle: Birds of Flight—Book Three
Falcon: Birds of Flight—Book Four
Flight of the Black Swan

Action/Adventure Science Fiction

Future Prometheus I: Emergence & Evolution—Novellas I & II
Future Prometheus II: Revolution, Successions & Resurrections—Novellas III, IV & V
Intelligent Design: Revelations
Intelligent Design: Apocalypse
The Prince: Lucifer's Origins
Future Prometheus: The Series
Intelligent Design: Revelations to Apocalypse
Rogue Event: Novella
To See Behind Walls
Time is for Dragonflies and Angels

...At most, terrestrial men fancied there might be other men upon Mars, perhaps inferior to themselves and ready to welcome a missionary enterprise. Yet across the gulf of space, minds that are to our minds as ours are to those of the beasts that perish, intellects vast and cool and unsympathetic, regarded this earth with envious eyes, and slowly and surely drew their plans against us. And early in the twentieth century came the great disillusionment ...

H.G. Wells, *The War of the Worlds*

Chapter One

Arcadia Planitia, Mars, 63 million years ago...

"JUST BEAUTIFUL. UNUSUALLY QUIET, but beautiful nonetheless." Master Architect Janus stood on his balcony, gazing over the miles of well-maintained but desolate homes in his nearempty city. The lots, arranged in neat rows, contained two to three-story rectangular homes interspersed with gardens and small farms. The Originators had constructed the planet's cities to accommodate twenty million inhabitants with privacy and space. The arrangement of well-marked roads, arboretums and gardens made the Martian landscape aesthetically simple and pleasing, well designed in both form and function. Canals laid out in a grid pattern ran throughout the plateau, their order in stark contrast to the irregularity of the occasional rivers that cut across the land. Four-story pyramids glimmered throughout the cityscape. Strategically placed by the waterways, they provided decentralized energy generation via water and solar.

The sun set, plunging the planet into a reddish blue twilight, and birds flew squawking from their nests in search of their evening meal.

"Not much food, I fear, for the birds of prey," Janus said. "It does sadden me that while we were able to collect the majority of the planet's species over the past century, we are leaving many behind." He leaned on the balcony railing and took another sip of coffee from his high-grade plastic mug.

Two birds took flight from a rooftop and swooped on a small pack of rodent omnivores that had become more daring in the absence of Martians and other prey. The birds seized one of the smaller rodents, but the rodent pack turned on the attackers. One of the birds barely escaped. The other lifted the struggling rodent into the sky.

That was close. There will be no love lost when that species disappears, Janus thought while watching the rodent pack reorganize and move onto an unsuspecting garden. He turned and took a slow step from the silence of the outside world into his office, where a low but constant flow of computer voices reciting different data streams, observations, and conclusions played over the office intercom just as they had for centuries. No seats surrounded the large empty work tables in the center of the room, but benches lined the surrounding walls along with potted vegetation, bound books, paper star charts, planetary models, and a sea of color-coded tablets. One uneaten plate of food, a bottle of wine, and an empty glass sat on a bench amongst analytical equipment and paperbound records.

Janus sauntered over to the bottle of wine and poured himself another drink. "Ah, Keeper, once again it is you and me, a handful of other stubborn old scientists, soldiers and the old left," he said just loud enough to be heard above the computer voices. "It is sad that after a millennium of preparation, I still wonder if we did everything we could to preserve life in this quiet corner of the galaxy."

He closed his layered work robes over his tall, thin frame and, with a full glass in hand, walked around his office, listening to the planet's master computer running billions of computations on the planet, colonies, and the solar event poised to happen at any moment. The master computer's female baritone stood out from the other computer tones as unmistakably in charge of the entire artificial intelligence of the planet.

"Master Architect Janus, I wish you would reconsider evacuating with the others. Both the Venus Keeper and the junior Architect of Earth request you join them. Your demise here is not necessary and it ... it pains me that you will not leave when you could live," the Keeper said in its resonant, feminine voice.

Hmm ... the beginning of emotion? Maybe she will survive and even reach sapience, he thought as he reviewed the number of cryogenic stasis chambers below. Though he had made his decision to stay long ago, he nodded as if he were actually considering it.

"No. I have no offspring, no spouse and no relatives. I have been in this workspace for two hundred years and in the field for another hundred years. I took over for Master Architect Lucius, who took over for Master Architect Guiana. They were of this world just as you are, Keeper. I can not leave this world any more than you can. And besides, are there not cryogenic stasis chambers well below the surface?" He sipped his wine.

"Experimental. The liquid bonding and temperature only preserved the last subject for thirty-two thousand annual rotations," the master computer said.

"Only thirty-two thousand rotations? That's quite a bit of time. Experimental? What are your metrics for success? A billion annual rotations? Your demand for perfection surpasses even my predecessors, and we know how Architect Lucius was."

"Yes ... Master Architect Lucius was demanding, critical and often correct even when his ideas were unconventional and far from the norm, but I digress. Please, Master Architect Janus, a ship awaits you to leave at any moment. I can report on the final days and moments here should they come as expected. The ship is designed for long range, long term cryogenic sleep. You can join the others who left long ago to find the Originators." She spoke with more emotion than he expected.

Persistent, and single-minded ... Impressive. "No, Keeper. Enough of this unresolvable discussion. When the time comes, I will, with the others, retreat to the chambers for safekeeping. " He walked towards the balcony, his mind racing again as thoughts of things to do and check on flowed through his head.

"By the way," he said, "I'm curious that with all my planning and efforts to salvage this solar system, why did you take it upon yourself to attempt to terraform Terra along with Junior Architect Hades? Why would you move ahead with such an unlikely plan on that tidal-locked planet, closer to hell than hope? If I did not know better, I would have guessed that Architect Lucius was still milling around here, or that he left a hidden program." He gazed out the balcony window and sipped his wine, hoping that his efforts to distract the master computer worked. The computer background voices and the quiet dialogue of internal programs on the intercom comforted rather than distracted him after all their years together. Yet, ironically, his one voice easily distracted his longtime master computer, colleague and friend.

"While primary efforts to relocate the majority of our indigenous species to Venus while we transform Terra are running well ahead of schedule, Earth's indigenous life has made it difficult to relocate the excess there. The massive warm-blooded omnivores have made havoc of our efforts, and the air quality still needs work, though minimal. Effort to transform Terra is low on the list but necessary should Earth not be a viable place for the excess overflow from Venus ..." the Keeper said.

Janus interrupted her. "So you allowed Architect Hades to create a warehouse on a planetary scale. Based on the manifests of terraform equipment and fission producers, there is more than enough power to simply heat a contained environment along the terminal line rather than create a habitable world. Am I right?"

"Yes. But Junior Architect Hades is young and ambitious. He did, in fact, keep your ideas as a backup plan should things go awry. However, like many his age, he prefers to dream big and take risks."

"And he took the rodents and their favorite mushrooms to Terra? Was this part of an experiment or does he have a fondness for fanged, long-scaled, tailed omnivores and fungi?" He watched the rodents methodically ravage the unattended garden.

"Architect Hades has taken a number of species, animal and vegetable, to see which species could exist underground in harsh conditions and darkness. He believes he can orchestrate an ecosystem where he can create a source of food, the omnivorous rodents, for higher order species should the proposed food chains collapse, such as a planetary disruption to food transports, supplies and commerce."

"Smart for sure but dangerous—the fungi and rodents will multiply and live anywhere. He would be better served to focus on transforming and let those species die out." Janus found it difficult to conceal his natural dislike for both species. He cringed at the thought of needing to eat either one if necessary. "I suppose there's also a good reason why Hades collected every large scale holographic emitter on our planet? Does he have any idea how the public would've responded if they were here to witness this act? They are difficult to construct and more difficult to move. I suppose I should be grateful he left mine alone."

"Architect Hades is convinced that with a continuous supply of energy the holographic emitters will bend light just beyond our visual range."

Janus calculated the creativity required and the probability of success in converting holographic emitters from projecting light particles to bending them and pushing them to either end of the light spectrum. After a moment, he chuckled.

"Once again, creative. He would need to utilize a power source as great as the terraform equipment, but he could do it. Risky, but he could cloak physical objects on a planetary scale, especially with Terra's dark side of ice as a reflector. Provided he doesn't blow up the the planet. Very risky."

"Yes."

But why he would want to do this? Because he can? Was I that foolish when I was young?

"Speaking of taking risks, please remind Architect Iris to slow down her titration of the Venetian atmosphere. I am concerned she's moving too quickly and could inadvertently create a runaway greenhouse effect. That would be bad." He stood, taking in the sight of his Martian home, and thought of something else to convey to Iris, about another young ambitious Junior Architect.

"She has been warned repeatedly on this matter ... Wait. Wait. Architect Janus, please look ..." Janus heard the Keeper speak, but the sky already drew his attention. A brilliant light filled the Martian twilight and, as it faded, a few lights flickered on in the empty cityscape—the homes of those citizens who had decided to stay. Janus took a deep breath, and his shoulders and the top of his back relaxed as if they'd been waiting for this moment, this catastrophic, extinction-level event.

"I take it the planets Gemini Alpha and Beta finally collided. I expected it to happen next month, thought their gravity wells might survive this pass. How their orbits became suddenly destabilized in the first place is beyond me, just as it was to my predecessors." Janus calmly continued to watch the light fade and the sky return to its darkening reddish blue tint.

"Not all the predecessors. Master Architect Guiana believed that it was 'the will and hand of the Originators,' though she lacked scientific support," the master computer said.

"It was her faith, Master Computer, not science that provided her answer, the answer that satisfied her to the last days of her life. Still, I thought there might be a little more time ..."

"Your assessment is accurate. In regards to the early destruction of the planets, it was the extreme gravitational pull of the twin planets' close proximity that ripped their cores apart. Our sensors have captured dramatic images of each planet's final moments. I will forward these events and recordings to the Keepers. The others will appreciate the scientific significance of this rare occurrence."

Though the Master Keeper's artificial intelligence often precluded emotion, Janus thought he detected emotion in her voice—sadness. *Our time is close to an end and another story is about to begin without us.* "Even with all our advanced technology, we could not keep the planets from destroying themselves."

"It was not through lack of trying," she said.

Janus smiled and started to take another sip of wine but stopped with a sigh at the compassion in her voice. *If only there was more time ...* "I'm guessing that extinction level debris will hit us in three days." He wasn't afraid. He, like everyone else, knew the end was coming. They'd had years to choose whether to leave or stay, and he'd decided, like Hades, the junior architects, all of them, to witness this phenomenon and see if they could save the viable worlds. Most left, few stayed. He'd made peace with his decision years ago.

"Unknown. It will take less than a minute to determine a timetable and where we will be hit. The impact craters will be impressive. Even with the debris on the other side of the Jovian planets, I speculate, based on their size and number of strikes, that nothing will survive on our planet's surface. I am also concerned based on the timing of this collision that Earth may be in the line of impact. Venus should be clear and the Sun will easily protect Terra," the Keeper said.

"That's ironic. The least habitable planet is safely protected behind the sun while Earth's monsters rule the planet, but ... if a series of meteors large enough to wipe out the species but not destroy the atmosphere struck ... it would give a narrow opening to transport mammalian life to Earth after the initial fallout."

"The gravitational disturbances could affect Terra's orbit as well as ours. They could alter the planetary axis as well, changing the climates and biosphere of each planet in unique ways."

"Yes ... the effects of a massive impact may eliminate the dinosaurs and provide an opportunity for new, more viable sapient life similar to our own," Janus said.

"Architect Iris will take full advantage of that," the master computer added.

"But no rodents or fungi ... please tell Hades to spare the planet." He turned from the balcony and marched to the center of his office, wondering if his sarcasm would be lost on the computer. "If your data collection is complete, please simulate the destruction of the Gemini planets with a projection of debris field, trajectory and the inner and outer planets' orbits," he said.

Within seconds, the architect's simple office mutated into a star field with the planetary bodies of Earth, Mars and Venus in position around the sun while images of the Jovian planets, Jupiter and Saturn with all of their moons, hovered in front of him. Just beyond them, two small planets close in mass to Mercury and in different orbital planes looked as if they would miss a collision. A sudden explosion of light sent a shock wave of debris in all directions.

"The energy released from their collision is impressive," Janus said.

"Yes."

"And based on the positioning of the Jovian planets, most of the debris will strike Jupiter and Saturn."

"But not all of the debris. Those planets' mass will pull in a substantial portion, but Earth, Venus and our world are exposed."

"And Terra is behind the sun."

"Yes."

"Maybe just enough debris ... end simulation," Janus said. The solar system dissolved around him and, once again, he stood in a simple office. After a moment of reflection, he strode to one of the desks.

"Based on your rate of walking and accelerated heart rate and blood pressure, I am guessing that you are revisiting transforming Earth based on the possibility that its life might be destroyed?" the Keeper asked.

"Yes."

"It is possible that should the dinosaurs survive, they might evolve into sapience, similar to mammals."

"Possible. But, based on computer projections, I believe Earth's atmosphere is slowly choking them into extinction. This cataclysmic event could clear the planet for another attempt for another species," he said as ideas flooded his mind.

When Janus stepped in front of his workstation, four monitors emerged from below the desk: and two keyboards and two stacked tablets appeared from a concealed drawer. Simultaneously, the other desks revealed various sized monitors, elaborate displays of key tasks and holographic images suspended in space. He looked at each screen in turn. They recognized his retina and gaze, and started sorting through various programs.

"Right now those carnivorous monsters will destroy everything that is smaller and unarmed. And while Terra might be out of harm's way from asteroids and the debris field, the heliosynchronous orbit that keeps it out of Earth's view might change in the course of millions of years. But that's for you to see should you and the other Keepers survive," he said absently as numbers and equations flooded his head.

"Sadly, unless I am able to perfectly titrate the cryogenic plasma solution, preserving you and the others for that long will be impossible. I will need a DNA sample when you have a chance. You do not much care for these dinosaurs, especially the carnivorous ones. You know they did not evolve from our rodents?" the Keeper said with more than an inflection of humor; something Janus would have considered thoroughly had he more time.

But why does she need a DNA sample? "Yes, I don't care much for dinosaurs or rodents. And we only have three days before we're destroyed, so we'd better get started."

His hands flew between the key boards and the monitors flashed with different graphs, equations, columns of numbers and maps. Images changed with a look at the monitor and a gesture of his eyes.

"Of course, if you leave now, you would be able to see the project through after our demise and keep the novice architects focused on their duties for years to come," the Keeper said.

"I'm impressed with your persistence." Though not surprised, Janus smiled at the fact that his master computer said nothing in response. "If the stasis chamber works, I might be revived someday to see the results first hand," Janus said to fill the void, while considering the material he needed to figure out his ecological problem.

"Perhaps, should the stasis chambers, underground power sources, control mechanisms, and the planet's crust survive the impacts."

Janus began to draw up plans for a Keeper on Earth. "I will leave if you do, Keeper."

"You know I am unable to leave this world; I am a part of it. While there can be records and images of me, I cannot be removed and relocated due to my connection to Mars."

"And that's the same reason I will stay. My roots are here, on Mars, in this room, with you, doing my work. Even in certain death there is hope for new life."

"I assume your response is an emotional construct that is not amenable to logical debate," the Keeper said.

"You are accurate." The Master Architect began to think of yet another opportunity that could spring from the approaching disaster.

Chapter Two

THIS IS SUCH BULLSHIT! Andrea Perez thought. Arms and legs folded, Perez had spent two hours sitting in a twelve by twelve spartan interview room with two silent federal agents. The growls of her hunger pangs pierced the silence, and she regretted not eating her chocolate glazed donut or the cinnamon muffin before she'd set her experiment. The simple experiment had involved light beams, prisms, ice, and new experimental holographic equipment sent by MIT. While it had taken hours to set up, the test would have taken only twenty seconds to complete had the school's dean not shown up with the department chair and three agents flashing badges and spewing the words 'national security.' She hadn't thought to take her food on the way out. It didn't seem like a viable option at the time, and it wasn't as if she were in any danger of starvation.

At least she had her good lab coat on; the others were too small and stained with everything from grit and oil to pizza sauce.

The doorknob turned for the first time in two hours, and Perez spun around, eager to hear a voice, any voice, but preferably one that would tell her what was going on. So far, she'd only had the sound of the fluorescent lights and her stomach to keep her company.

An older man in full military dress entered the room. "Dr. Perez? Thank you for waiting. I know this is a little out of the ordinary, but I think after the meeting you'll understand the necessity."

Tall, physically fit and with very nice blue eyes, 'older' may have been too much. *Seasoned maybe; mature.*

"Let me guess: national security reasons."

"Exactly."

"What's really going on here?" Perez demanded as she stood. "You don't have the right to hold me. Why did these guys take me out of my lab?"

"I know it must seem odd to you."

"No … why would it be odd? Three FBI dudes show up at my lab, flash their badges and whisk me away. And the dean and department head just keep saying 'don't worry,' as they wave me off. Who are you people, and what do you want?"

"Please, Dr. Perez …"

"I'm not a doctor! I'm a doctoral student. What the hell?"

The soldier held up his hands as if surrendering. "Okay. Please sit down, Ms. Perez, and I'll explain everything."

Perez stopped and consciously unclenched her fists and jaw. She took a deep breath and sat. Another loud, protracted hunger pain broke the silence. After two hours of sitting in a small, blank office with two silent FBI men who were totally unresponsive to any questions, her blood was boiling. An image of her dad flashed in her mind along with a sudden sense of concern. He was a military man who practiced clinical work with the Veterans Administration.

"Does this have something to do with my dad? What do you want from him? He's had enough shit happen and doesn't need to be pulled into anything you people have to offer." Perez sat away from the small table with her arms folded and her legs crossed; her body language made it clear she was not happy to be in the room. The officer shook his head and sat on the chair opposite her, then took off his cap and pulled his seat into the desk. He made eye contact with the FBI agents and they moved towards the door.

Perez locked her eyes on the new arrival and spoke in an even, sarcastic tone. "Hey, guys? Thanks for the conversation. Let's do it again soon."

To their credit, they left the room as silent as they had been for hours.

Who the hell are these people? Tension tightened her shoulders, neck and arms. Even her face felt tight.

"Again, I apologize for the secrecy and the strange way we had to move, but it was necessary to ensure that we secure your work so you can continue …" the man said.

"I'm not talking to you or anyone until I have a name and a clear explanation of why I was brought here against my will and without reason. I want to know, right now." She kept her tone low and calm, but anger laced every word.

"I will explain everything, Ms. Perez. As crazy as it will sound, I'll tell you everything, but please let me finish before you ask any questions. Once you hear everything, you'll have to figure out what questions to ask, because once you find out what's going on, you'll grab your balls." Perez's eyes widened at the mention of what she would grab, and she fought to keep a smirk off her face.

The officer's face flushed and he spoke quickly to recover his equanimity. "My name is Lieutenant Colonel David Farrell. I run the communication, spectrographic analysis and guidance division of NASA's space exploration and the search for intelligent life. My job covers a lot of areas, and I work with a lot of brilliant scientists around the world—China, Russia, India, and any other country, no matter how small, that has a telescope, computer and bright people."

Spectrographic analysis? There's a whole department that looks at light? And here I thought I was the only nut looking at it.

"As you can imagine, working on such areas with different governments can be difficult, but in this case it's necessary." Farrell broke eye contact and looked at his hands.

Perez noticed the change, something her father always told her to look for when people were talking. Was it a mark of anxiety, or an indication that he was hiding something?

"You know, Ms. Perez, we live in a world of dualities. On one hand, we have technology that can pick up chemical compositions of planets outside our solar system, and we can now grow and transplant human organs. There are space probes in deep, interstellar space, and we can tell when and how many times our planet wobbles on its axis," he said, still looking at his hands. "At the same time, there's a cult in Ireland who believe there are aliens living among us. In another part of the world, we have a madman who's president of a powerful country looking to retake former territories in an effort to rebuild an empire. Finally, we have a pandemic of religious violence to determine once and for all whose god is the most just and benevolent."

Perez frowned. Confusion, a feeling she loathed, and frustration at his digression replaced her anger. "What does this have to do with me?"

Farrell held up his hand to stop her. It did, but he stayed silent for a few seconds before he spoke again.

"Ever since Galileo looked at the stars, we knew there were other worlds out there. Other giant minds came, and they were able to pinpoint where we fell in our constellation, how our planet's orbit affected our world, and where to look for new discoveries. When the space age started, we led the charge into space. The *Apollo* missions, *Luna 16, Mariner 10*, *Spirit* and *Opportunity, Voyager*, *Messengers, New Horizons*, all of them, and many more you and the public don't know about, all set out to chart, investigate and discover everything at our front door and beyond. When we look out, there are so many possibilities in other galaxies. And when we look close to home, we find that Mars once held an atmosphere and water, and a couple of moons near Jupiter and Saturn hold possibilities for life. Nothing else, or so we thought." Farrell's voice trailed off as if he were thinking of something to add.

Perez listened to every word, so focused on what he said that her body unfurled and leaned on the desk towards him, waiting for him to continue.

"Over the past thirty-five years, we've picked up unusual variations in our orbit and other small changes in Mars and Venus. They were minute at first but clearly there. In the last ten years, this variation has become predictable, measurable, and clearly indicative that a large body of something out there is affecting our planet's orbit. Nothing dangerous, but clearly there is another factor, on a planetary scale."

The room fell silent. Perez noted her shallow breathing, took a deep breath, and shook her head as if to break some kind of spell. "No way! Are you drunk? Is this some kind of psychological game or an elaborate joke Dr. Vincent came up with?" Perez wiped a hand across her suddenly hot and sweaty brow.

Farrell continued as if she had said nothing. "Fifteen years ago, a series of probes and satellites were sent to specific coordinates to observe this disturbance. That's after we reviewed millions of images, new and old, from all the probes, missions, and satellites from every country capable of space flight. We found nothing, or rather we *saw* nothing, nothing visual occupying the space we pinpointed. Direct observation was initiated and the *Veritas* probes were launched. When the first one got to its designated location, we lost all contact. When the second and third got into place, all seemed to work well until they initiated spectral analysis and x-rays, then they went dark. The third probe did send back data, and for just a nanosecond we thought we had something, but then some kind of computer glitch happened, and the data was lost. The fourth *Veritas* probe blew up on the launch pad," Farrell added more to himself than to her.

"You're not joking, are you?"

"No. No, I'm not."

Holy shit ...

Farrell looked at her. "We re-routed a couple of satellites and old probes to our mystery disturbance, but they experienced some kind of problem or their data was useless for some reason or other. China and Russia experienced the same problems. And now, for the last eight years, the internet is alive with chat groups and forums talking about 'Planet X' on the far side of the sun."

"They're in on this too?"

"Yup. They got similar results."

"Jesus ..."

"The South Koreans successfully launched their own probe. They were able to shoot a light beam in the general direction of the anomaly and got a measure of curvature before it went dark."

"Curvature? The light bent?"

"Yes. The light's particles curved as if affected by a large planetary body. When the curvature of the light beam was measured, it was extrapolated that only a planet larger than Earth would have the gravity to do that."

Stunned, Perez looked directly at Farrell. He held her gaze and continued.

"We have another set of probes getting ready to launch in the next four years with an array of spectrograph equipment and an unparalleled number of telescopes and measuring devices. In addition, we're establishing a manned launch so we can have direct human observation. All of this in spite of a major economic downturn, a recession that will dwarf the Great Depression. We are doing this as we exit two wars, and the danger from terrorism and maniacal leaders lurks everywhere. A world of dualities."

"If all our satellites, probes and shit haven't been able to see it or snap an image, what will sending people to observe do?" Perez's anxiety had kicked into high gear, and sweat broke out on her forehead, armpits and small of her back.

"We're not going to just look for it. We're beyond that now. Everything points to something being out there. And whatever it is, a massive asteroid, planetoids, moon or whatever, we're going to land on it and bring a piece of whatever it is home."

"You're going to ... to land on an invisible planet?"

"There's something out there. If it's real, we can land on it."

Perez blinked. Her eyes and throat felt dry. It might have been only two minutes of silence, but it seemed longer before Perez continued. "There can't be another planet in our solar system. We'd have seen it. It's just not possible."

"I've been doing this job for too long, Ms. Perez. There's been a lot of smart people, a huge amount of money and technology thrown at this, and yet the mathematics and physics don't lie: there is something as big as a planet on the other side of our Sun that's ducking us. And when I mean it's ducking us, I mean it's actively hiding. Either it exists at a spectrum of light we just don't see naturally or it's artificially created to keep us from seeing it."

"No, no, no ... Now you're talking science fiction, or an advanced civilization or technologically gifted species that's hanging out in our solar system. Come on!"

"Absolutely, Ms. Perez, and it's here, too, on Earth."

"What? It can't be ..."

"It's all true. When we've been able to get data to our servers and computers, there's always some kind of data incompatibility issue or information degradation that makes the information, images, everything useless. And government sponsored projects to advance surveillance have had their imaging and spectrograph equipment destroyed, hindered, or blocked. Ultimately, their plans disappear or are so badly altered that they too are useless."

Perez held up her hands as if trying to slow the conversation and its inevitable train wreck.

"Colonel, what you're saying is ... well, it's just too incredible. I mean, it means there's some kind of world just beyond our line of sight that's able to bend light waves so it's invisible. And now you're saying there's some kind of conspiracy as well. That someone's messing with our technology to make sure we don't see what's there." Saying it all out loud did not make it sound less crazy as Perez had hoped. "Do you hear yourself?"

"Sure do. Have for years. It takes a while to believe, but when you and others say the same thing all the time, it becomes as real as it gets."

"A conspiracy on Earth too?"

He answered without hesitation. "Absolutely. All your notes, designs, and all electronically-stored documentation of your project disappeared this morning."

Perez was on her feet in milliseconds. *Years of research, thousands of hours work, all gone!* "What? Are you bullshitting me! That's not remotely funny!"

To Farrell's credit, he remained calm and still, and allowed for the burst of emotion to pass as if he had been in that very situation before. After a moment, he nodded and motioned for her to sit down. Once she'd settled and her heart rate had slowed, he spoke in the therapeutic tone her father had used to calm his clients.

"Yes, Ms. Perez. All your work saved on the university's server system, external backup system and cloud started to degrade into an unintelligible mess or disappear altogether. Since we've been monitoring your work, we saw it happening, re-routed and manually inputted some of your backup files to old thumb drives. We also dispatched the local bureau to pick you up before anything happened to you."

Shit.

Farrell looked at his hands again.

"What do you mean?" Perez asked. "What happens to the people that do what I do or make advances on this problem?" She sat in her chair with her arms folded over her chest, very aware of her clothes absorbing her sweat.

He replied immediately. "They disappear, fall off the planet. Even their electronic footprint disappears as if they were never here. Even when they're in protective custody, or witness protections, they still disappear. INTERPOL and Scotland Yard have been all over this for the last three years. The lead guy at Scotland Yard is convinced there's something systemic, so tied into our computer systems that we are missing something."

"Maybe he's wrong …"

"Bradley? Arthur Bradley from Scotland Yard? Wrong?" Farrell said with more emotion than she had heard for the entire interview. "Bradley is many things, but he's not wrong here. He's the guy who found the patterns with the computer and people disappearances. No, he's not wrong. I wish he was."

More silence. Throat dry and breathing deeper, Perez thought she would have more questions but only managed one. "What happens next?"

"We're going to go into the next room where there are a bunch of stenographers using old manual stenotype machines and scientists with pens and pads of paper that are going to write everything you say about your project down. Your work is remarkable and that's why we're moving fast. If the data breach's speed is any indicator, your work may hold the key in seeing the invisible," Farrell replied.

After a moment of silence, Perez could hear the fluorescent light again in addition to her breathing. Her growling hunger pains had gone. "A whole planet? An entire world just outside the visible spectrum?"

"Yup, and that's not the interesting part."

"What? A whole planet next door and we can't see it, and that's not the interesting part? Jesus, Colonel! What's enough to pique your interest?"

"I don't think invisible planets occur naturally. Who's running the technology to make an entire planet invisible and why are they hiding?" Farrell returned to looking at his folded hands.

"What happens to me after I give you everything?"

"You go into witness protection. A place where there's lots of wheat fields, in the middle of nowhere. No computer or internet. Just books, lots of books if you like."

Perez sat still. Her world and life had completely changed in mere hours.

Shit.

Chapter Three

COLD RAIN WASHED OVER Andrea Perez. She stood, feeling chilled and drenched, in the middle of a cornfield with her slipper-clad feet sinking into the mud. A huge, black bird-shaped ship hovered silently mere feet above the ground.

Three small females stood before her. Their sleek black jumpsuits seemed at odds with their large jaws, sloping foreheads, and broad faces. "Obviously, we are not from around here," the redhead said.

"I thought aliens would have really big heads and speak telepathically?"

"Why do Earthers say that when it is clear that they are the giants? But enough. For you to be safe, we must go," the woman said. No coercion, no force, just a statement.

Still, she hesitated. "Safe? From who? Farrell?"

"No, not him. He is determined and committed to the truth, but he means you no harm. Others are not like him. And if we were able to find you with ease, they surely will."

"My dad? He'll be alone?"

"No, he will not. He understands and wishes you well. He will join you but not before his work is done."

"What work?"

"Preparing Earth for the truth. We need your help as well."

"Why me?"

"Our holographic emitters are failing. We need your help."

Reassured, Perez smiled and approached the ship's extended ramp with confidence. "I'll miss the rain," she said.

Why will I miss the rain ... there's no rain on Terra?

Lightning. Ice. Caves. Underground ... There's only rain on Earth. I'm not on Earth.

Perez's consciousness returned as her recurring dream of her last day on Earth faded. She sat up, jolted to the present. She'd had far too many mushrooms and 'special' cabbage dishes that, though they filled her quickly, made her very sleepy. After years of combining those two foods, she should expect such dreams.

Perez blinked and stretched in her seat. She'd fallen asleep at her work station in her small quarters. A series of old blueprints for terraform equipment that had been converted to energy for the Terran community's life support systems and holographic emitters lay on the table. The first thing she'd done when she'd arrived was to recommend periods of taking the cloaking field offline when Earth satellites and probes weren't around. She found it ironic that she was one of the key conspirators on a hidden planet that Farrell had alluded to so many years ago. Now, fully awake in the present, she noticed a water stain where her head had been, right beside her empty plate and cup. She wiped her mouth. Yes, she'd drooled as she slept. "Now, that's really unattractive," she muttered.

Though still dressed in her plain brown slacks, and black and reddish tunic, she wanted to pull off her shoes and crawl into bed just feet away. Her quarters had been built for women of less than five foot three; she was lucky to have two rooms and her own semi-private bathroom with attached bathing area.

"Just when you thought college dorm life was bad." Her knife, affixed at her waist, gave her the feeling that she had to be somewhere else—she only took a weapon when leaving her quarters.

She glanced at the piles of large books, tablets, and paper charts stacked like pyramids around the room. A flash of Terra's spinning molten core, unusual on a tidal-locked planet, popped into her head. She often wondered how a still planet could generate such a powerful magnetic field solely by the planet's core. It was fascinating how Terra's spacecraft used magnetic fields for landings and launches.

"Wait! The launch! Crap!"

Perez raced out the door and into the narrow common hall in a bid to make her appointed time. Low lights ensconced and scattered throughout the residence core allowed her to see and wave back to her neighbors and coworkers, who all lived next to each other in a honeycomb structure made of stone.

"Late for another meeting, Perez?" an unusually large-jawed woman said with an even larger grin.

"Thanks for overstating the obvious, Hydra!"

She wove in and out of small pockets of people, all with pale white skin and dark brown eyes. Being a full head taller than her new peers made her stick out in a crowd, and even after all her years here, she still wasn't used to her lean body. If she exercised as Clematis had suggested, she would become even fitter, could perhaps even become an athlete.

Once the first of three flights of stairs came into view, she no longer needed signs to guide her through the elaborate community. She sprinted up the staircase as a siren began to screech. The sound of spinning turbines and other machinery hummed constantly throughout the subterranean world, and periodic sirens marked changes of shifts, announcements, and, rarely, warnings. This siren proclaimed a shift change that meant in a few seconds mobs of people would fill the corridors, preparing either to arrive for their shift or to go home, eat, dance or hunt.

Her breath grew ragged and her leg muscles tightened with the effort, but she was determined not to miss her meeting. "Not again ... I swear I won't hear the end of it."

A group of scientists, identified by their green sashes, gathered just ahead of her. They waved their tablets and spoke with great enthusiasm, while just behind her, another group carried sharpened spikes, spears and other edge weapons for a hunt.

"You'd think … that with all the advanced technology … they'd have invented elevators or escalators," she gasped while running up her third flight of stairs. Though not completely out of breath yet, her hope that she'd reach Legate Legionis Clematis and Dux Cloelius dwindled.

I bet they're already gone. What the hell, Perez. Lay off the vegetables and mushrooms!

Despite almost fifteen years of acclimating to her new home, Terra's gravity still strained her human body. Terra was only slightly larger than Earth, considered by most of her peers as negligible, but they didn't have to live with the change for the rest of their lives. She wondered if she'd live beyond a hundred like these people—more time to learn more languages, origins and maybe even find a new power source for the emitters.

Perez, comfortable now with the array of edged weapons and firearms they carried nearly all the time in their subterranean world, dodged more clusters of females clad in various browns, black and reddish colors. Her own knife bounced against her hip.

Damn! Forgot my sidearm again! I'll regret that one of these days.

She entered a larger space brightened by light reflected through large skylights. Unique markets, food dispensaries, drinking establishments and places to sit lined the sides of a wide foyer. Though reminiscent of the old markets of Earth, the ornate, colorful sculptures, free standing or embedded in large stone archways, resembled those of ancient Rome. But while ancient Rome had fallen on Earth, here, Rome's origins and life remained commonplace.

So much to learn still, she thought as she sidestepped a group of adolescents and avoided crashing into a weapons rack. Edged weapons were so familiar in public that she hardly noticed the first aid kits, fire extinguishers, atmosphere alarms, and racks of knives for killing the planet's large rodents.

I really have to learn more maneuvers, she thought as she continued her jaunt past more newly installed racks. The monsters had become more brazen recently.

Finally, she saw the two women. They'd stopped to wait for her in the congested walkways. She realized that with an entire civilization built underground—three level structures on the surface and three below the crust—elevators for people were not really necessary. Feeling as tall as a giraffe in the land of lions, she could easily spot the Terran-Earth mixed children. Even as adolescents, they were taller than the native Terran. Perez enjoyed her transition into a society that valued height and strength almost as much as teaching and learning. As a scientist and an ambassador from Earth, she held the title of Immunes, a direct derivation from Latin meaning a soldier with at least one specialization. Her pink sash, one of five on the whole planet, indicated the high regard in which they held her—a scientist responsible for fixing a failing cloaking system for the planet.

New arrivals from different parts of Terra looked sideways at her; even though the proportions of her limbs and trunk were nearly identical to theirs, they perceived her Earthly thick build and short stature as thin and tall. Her thick, dark-brown hair, which fell below her shoulders, was truly an anomaly among the shorter red-haired women and the few Terran men. Her narrower head with a corresponding jaw, higher cheek bones and an average human skull with its high forehead all differed from her Terran counterparts with their heavier brows, sloping foreheads, and flatter craniums that jutted out more towards the back of the neck. But what really turned heads was her brown skin, signifying her heritage from Earth's sub-Saharan Africa, along with her European-genus blue eyes. These features indicated that she came from a world where one could be in the sun without fear of immediately dying.

"In the land of the blind, the one-eyed giant will be king," she remembered her dad often said. *I wonder if this is about him? Have they moved up the plans? It really would be great to see him sooner than later.*

Finally, she stood before the women and bent over to catch her breath. Her original assessment of being out of shape dissolved as she realized she'd run at least a mile in about nine minutes. Back on Earth when she was out of shape, she could've run half a mile in the same time, then would've promptly thrown up.

Legate Legionis Clematis and Dux Cloelius looked up from their stone-like tablets, one green and the other purple. "Minor Perez! We are so happy you made it." It hadn't taken Perez long to get used to the title 'minor' meaning younger. They referred to her dad as seniores. *He'd hate that.*

"You must have run to catch us. But I see you have neglected your sidearm. That is dangerous," Clematis said with a smile as she put her tablet in her tunic and planted her hands akimbo.

Cloelius produced a canteen of water and offered it to Perez. Clematis nodded in approval.

Perez straightened and took the canteen. "But ... but you never carry a firearm ... only knives..." she said between gasps of breath.

"That is because I've been battle tested. I killed two rattus with one spike and a spear. No need for me or Cloelius to carry a firearm. Someday, you will face the challenge, and it will be decided then," she said enthusiastically.

Perez drank the opaque liquid, a salty-sweet syrup mixture that both quenched thirst and gave energy. "I ... must ... catch my breath ... first."

She focused on her breathing and pushed the thoughts of large rats, or rattus as Terrans often called them, out of her head. *I think I'll stick to walking in well-lit, well-populated areas before I take that challenge,* she thought.

"You are a special one, Perez. But we must go. The launch dance is already in progress, and the Centurions and Milites have already boarded *Silent Star Falling.* They await our arrival." Clematis began their mile trek to the launch bay with Cleolius, Perez and other high-ranking officials in tow.

"There must have been a change in plans for the mission to be moved ahead to now." Perez handed Cloelius's canteen back with a thank-you nod and fell into step with the smaller officers, one a general and the other a leader, though she was still not sure who was who.

The military here had rank and order but no saluting, barking orders, or rigid behavior. Military order was somehow inbred as prescribed and predictable behaviors, part of their nature as a species. They had no need to remind each other.

Her father would love it here—a clinical person's dream come true. He would wish he'd pursued that anthropology course he started ... Her mind hit a dark wall. Her smile faded and her heart sank as her last memories of her mother and brother flooded her mind. Years after their deaths, her father had finally pulled out of his depression and attended some anthropology courses at a local college, something her mom had done when she was younger.

"Do not grieve, Perez. The Keeper of Atlantis believes she can ensure safe passage for your father to the extraction zone. She is just being cautious in moving it up. She wants to make sure she gets the supplies to us even though we have what we need for probably centuries to come. Nonetheless, I do hope she has provided your planet's chestnuts in the cargo. They are remarkable! How you humans simply let them grow on trees and fall to the ground is beyond me."

"Thank you for your reassurance." Perez followed the women through the crowd of people who stood or sat around the foyer, talking, laughing or singing in groups. Some peered into their own uniquely-colored tablets, and some told stories as they sharpened their weapons and drank a version of coffee.

They walked past multiple shops, but Perez no longer looked away from the skinned rattus hides that hung near the market place. Scaled tails with sharp edges at the ends, and their size—as large as dogs—distinguished them from the common Earth rat. They lived underground and were not only the primary source of meat protein but also, and more importantly, hunting them provided a way to prove yourself and advance in station and rank. Most Terran citizens survived their hunt for the *norvegicus rattus*, but some fell to the packs and never returned. And sometimes, the creatures would come up to the foyers and take a child or unsuspecting Terran. Hence, everyone always carried weapons. You could count on two things with Terrans: hunting and dancing, with rituals to match for every situation. *Just as you'd expect from cave dwellers!*

"I wonder why you Terrans love chestnuts so much," Perez said. "Does it have something to do with your Earthly ancestors? A kind of DNA-loaded thing that still lingers?"

"I do believe you're right, Perez," Cloelius replied. "There are many references made of them in the ancient articles, and our own Keeper has thoroughly explained what they are and the role they played in our development. Sadly, like so many things we left behind, chestnuts, bark and lemons... dogs are the ones I think we all miss the most."

Lemons? Yuck! "Not being outside? Being stuck in these caverns? I thought that would be the thing you'd miss the most."

Clematis took her time answering, just as all Terrans did.

"Maybe the open fields for the hunt, too, and tracking the herds, chasing them and finally capturing them. The rattus hiding in the depths of the caverns are not the same, for sure. But then the Keeper reminds us that there are places on the Earth where it is very cold, and the elements harsh, yet the Earthers live on the surface rather than embedded in the ground. I love it when our cloaking field is off, and we can view powerful storms from our underground world in safety, comfort and peace. And where day and light collide on the surface, we can watch Terra's beautiful twilight with wind and fire on the day side, and ice and lightning on the night side ... just glorious! A perfect place."

"Except for the rats." Perez felt for her sheathed knife as she eyed a very large rodent skin and tail hanging near a stove—possibly five feet long, with a full snout of teeth in its skull and an additional four feet of tail—truly a monster rat from hell. *Vile and disgusting.*

"Yes, except for them. Cunning, smart and clever," Clematis said with a smile.

Perez nodded and pushed the rodent image from her mind's eye. They navigated around even more people on the cavern's third story arboretum—an open design supported by huge stone columns and flavored by the smell of cooked meat and vegetables wafting up from the open market below. The increasing number of teenage males intermingling with the larger number of young women surprised and pleased Perez. The boys' reddish, dark hair and taller stature, the expected result of cross-breeding, made them easy to pick out. Efforts to replenish the male species seemed to be progressing better than expected.

The purplish sunlight of the never-ending Terran twilight filtered in from the narrow skylights above. With the planet tidal-locked with its sun, the inhabitable zone on planet Terra stretched across the terminal line of perpetual day and night. Perez had been in one of the few places on the planet where one could look over the surface, and the perfect positioning of the few exposed, low-lying buildings to seize solar energy for powering the holographic emitters had impressed her. Failing millions of years old machinery, not lack of sunlight, caused the problem.

Perez never thought she would miss day and night, but she did—rain too. She wondered what the Terrans would do if they experienced the total light of day and the darkness of night. She remembered that they'd really liked the rain.

"The Keeper asked us to bring extra rations for eight people, especially dried meat and fish products and preserves," Clematis said. "It saddens me that the Keeper will continue to stay on Earth even to the end. Her action is consistent with the Great Keeper. Unfortunately, her rationale does make sense. Of all the humans on your planet, she is sure your father has found one that can help the Earthers understand their predicament and maybe even our existence." Clematis helped Cloelius open the heavy doors that led to the busy walkway to the launch pad.

Heavy drums beating in the distance echoed through the cavern, and the closer they approached the next vaulted cavern, the louder it got.

Seriously ... Dancing and drums?

"I hope to talk to the Keeper, and my father, someday. But I suppose I'll need to take the journey to earn my own stone tablet, with my own color, I presume, before I can do that," Perez said.

Clematis smiled and nodded. "I suspect that your own curiosity and need to know will propel you on your journey without you even knowing it. You have been on many journeys and paths with your work and searching, but I think there is yet a bigger one you harbor."

Perez nodded as if she understood everything Clematis said, but she wished the Terrans would speak bluntly. *Why the riddles?* "It will be good to see my father, though, after all these years." Near the entrance to the launch pad, a group of soldiers and scientists moved in rhythm with the music, holding knives, swords and other spear-like weapons above their heads.

With the clash of modern technology and primal music, Perez was surprised not to find a roaring fire pit with one of those rodents cooking on a spit …

Yuck! Now that's an image I have to get out of my head. Good job, Perez!

Cloelius stopped at the opening to the launch bay. "I understand that your father has thoroughly embraced our natural diet and habits and can make this trip, though he still has difficulty with keeping step and dancing. Still, his ability to lift his own weight and to square off with Centurion Dea Data at his seasoned age is impressive, especially on Earth with all those poisons, distractions and dangers."

The humming and circular dancing of the families, soldiers, and scientists overshadowed even the powerful resonance of the beating drums. A group of Terran humans dressed in plain uniforms performed a tribal dance with edged weapons in hand, while a huge black spaceship in the shape of a raven stood on a launch pad in the middle of a cavern supported by huge stone columns. Pyramid-shaped buildings two to three stories high filled with still more scientists and flight specialists surrounded the ship. They held an uncanny resemblance to the significantly larger pyramids of Earth's Egypt, and she'd seen similar structures throughout Terra and along the terminal line on the surface. The Terrans had housed their holographic emitters in the same simple design, perfect for surviving the violent weather—fierce winds, explosive lightning, and constant thunder—of the tidal-locked planet. If it wasn't for the planet's powerful magnetic field, the surface of the planet would have long since been destroyed by solar winds and space debris.

"Perez?" Clematis said. "You have noticed these structures before and yet you have done no research as to their origin and why they appear on both your worlds."

Perez turned to face the woman and smiled at her words, confirmation that the Terrans truly accepted her as part of their world.

"You know, it'd be easier to simply tell me the origin of our worlds. Your practice of having your young and curious seek out their answers from the library themselves doesn't seem efficient, especially when I have no stone to access the Keeper." Perez tried to drown out the drums and public announcements. She already knew the answer Clematis would provide. Still, Perez enjoyed the shock she gave when she made such a bold statement.

"And deprive you and the curious of their journeys? Simply tell you? That confounds the process of truth. It would be quite a disservice to hinder one's natural growth that way. If we were at war or in danger, then it makes sense. But we have not been at war for thousands of years because each of us takes our own path to finding our place. We go as far as we wish, but we all go; we are not told. And based on my experience of you, Perez, I suspect you will go very far in your journey. If we have learned anything from the Earthers, it is that they do not do well with letting mysteries lie. They seek the truth at all costs—good for the seekers who stay on the path. The knowledge, however, is lost on those who simply observe without the benefit of taking the road to understanding." Clematis smoothed her tunic and adjusted her weapons, obviously preparing herself for something important.

"So I have to find my own answers … just like my dad would always say," Perez said.

"Yes."

Suddenly embarrassed that she had been on Terra for fifteen years and had learned only about its unique history, Perez decided to find out not just the origins of Terra and the planet's connection to Earth but also the origins of *everything* in her solar system, and to do it well before her father arrived.

She tried to cut herself some slack; after all, she was a stranger in a new, undiscovered world far from home and needed to find her place. She remembered her shock and awe when Lieutenant Colonel David Farrell had first told her of the possibility so many years ago … *I wonder how he's doing. I bet he'd like it here—kind of his type of people.*

"So be it," Perez said, more to herself than to Clematis. Her friend turned to her and smiled as widely as her large jaw would allow. The size of the Terran's jaw and teeth still amazed Perez. *No wonder they could eat chestnuts like peanuts.*

"Excellent! So you are beginning yet another journey. Great things you will find. Difficult at first but wonderful once you see the tapestry of it all." Clematis took a deep breath and walked towards the front of the waiting ship. Perez looked back for Cloelius and found her in the middle of one of the dancing rings. At the base of the ship, the centurion, captain of the vessel, stretched out her hands and cried, "*Datum est verbum?*"

Is the word given? Perez understood the phrase as requesting permission to depart. The centurion waited dutifully in her dark-red flight suit while the din of the drums and Terran voices escalated. Clematis stretched her arms above her head and belted out the expected phrase: "*Datur est verbum!*" *The word has been given.*

With that, the drums increased even more, the centurion retreated onto the ramp below the bird-shaped ship, and it closed as the launch pad's heavy mechanical gears and hydraulics slowly lifted the ship to the ceiling of the cavern, hundreds of feet above them.

Unbelievable … this never gets old.

The huge black ship rose silently in the air, looking like a falcon waiting to fly. After just a few minutes, while the dancing and drumming escalated even further, two large doors opened above the cavern. Wind flowed inside until the bottom of the launch pad sealed the opening with a loud clunk, leaving the ship on the surface. A minute later, the roar of engines carried through the reinforced metal launch pad and drowned out the sounds of drums and humans.

Cloelius came up behind her. "Perez? The pad will remain at the surface for a couple of hours to ensure that fuel residue, flames and vapors are cleared away by the atmosphere above."

A public announcement broke through the din, and the drumming and dancing stopped. "*Qui me fecit, stella cadens circulum. Deinde cum dicit: quod stella cadens tacita consequi orbis!*"

A burst of cheers erupted and the drumming and dancing resumed. Perez took her time to translate the literal meaning in her head: "Mission Leader, Leader Ennius reports that *Silent Star Falling* has achieved orbit. Repeat: *Silent Star Falling* has achieved orbit.' It is a great day for us all."

Perez glanced around. Everyone was getting into the music and dancing. She joined in, but struggled to keep in step with the shorter, red-headed, pale-skinned, dark-eyed Terrans. *Latin, German, French ... those were easy to learn. But dancing? I need more practice.*

Chapter Four

"...YOURS IS THE KINGDOM and the Power and the Glory, I of the Father, and of the Son, and of the Holy Spirit; both now and ever, and to the ages of ages. Amen."

Roberta Joanne Riesman refocused her attention to the priest's prayer. With so many prayers in a period of three hours, she had lost herself in thought.

"I knew so many things about him," she said softly. At forty-five, it wasn't her first funeral, not by a long shot, but it was the longest she'd ever experienced and the closest she'd endured in a long time.

"...Glory to the Father and to the Son and to the Holy Spirit.

"You are our God, who went down to Hades, to loosen the pains of the dead that were there; Give rest also to the soul of Your servant, O Savior ..."

She sniffled. There were so many things she didn't know about him.

Other wakes and funerals had moved her with their stories of a wonderful life, or a young soldier taken too soon. Last week, three firefighters in Yellowstone. *And next week? Does it matter?*

Her shoes sank in the moist grass. Dark skies hung about her with no likelihood of clearing. The empty trees, muffled sounds of restrained sobs and coughs made everything so real. For any other funeral, she could have gone for an early morning run to shake off the pain, but she knew she could run forever and the pain would persist. This was not a normal funeral.

"Hiaki ..."

Riesman wondered if the priest swinging incense around the closed casket indicated the end of the service. His low, somber voice drew her in and helped her hope that her lover had found peace. She had not and never would. Never again.

"...O God of all spirits and of every flesh, who did trod down death and overcome the devil, bestowing life on this Your world, to the soul of this Your servant, Hiaki Nakamura, departed this life, to You Yourself, O Lord, give rest in a place ..."

Riesman looked beyond the priest to a throng of darkly dressed family members and friends of Dr. Hiaki Nakamura, brilliant mathematician, statistician, and theorist. A mild-mannered soul whose warm gaze, kind eyes and soft smile had melted her heart years ago when he joined her team. After years of working with him, she'd found her vacations annoying and had joined him in the field whenever he headed to a disaster area. His voice, humor, eyes, and touch held her heart with no chance of escape. *He can't ... I just can't believe he's gone.*

"...establish the soul of His servant, Hiaki, departed from us, in the testings of the Just; give him rest in the bosom of Abraham; and number him among the Just, through His goodness and compassion as our merciful God." The priest finished with the incense and now held Mrs. Nakamura's hand, consoling her, while she and her two grown daughters stood by the closed casket. Still monitoring her own breathing, Riesman's hot tears fell again on her cheeks.

She found a well-worn tissue and wiped her eyes beneath her sunglasses. She didn't need them to block out the sun but to cover the bloodshot eyes that would betray the depths of her despair. He'd been more than a friend, just short of a soul mate. The weeping widow and two daughters with their families aroused a mixture of grief and guilt. In an effort to distract herself, she rewound her conversation with her administrative assistant around an hour ago.

He'd reported that the FBI seal flashed across Nakamura's computer screen, denying access. Hiaki's sudden death probably prompted the response. It wasn't unusual for them to confiscate computers when someone from FEMA or Homeland Security died as a result of an accident, but Hiaki's heart attack, while tragic, was of natural causes according to the reports. As to what was on the computer, they had shared more secrets than the average employer-employee, so its loss did not concern Riesman. Suddenly aware that she was staring at the family, she looked away. The priest had finished, and already a long line of people queued to bid their last farewell. If she hadn't been his boss, she would have left immediately.

You deserve better than that, Hiaki. I just wish we had more time.

One of her aides touched her gently, startling her from her thoughts. He held the umbrella for her and, with a nod, gestured her to move.

"Thank you, Peter."

Her aides and protection detail were quiet, respectful, and, most of the time, invisible. Just as she liked it. She wiped her eyes and cheeks again and scanned the surroundings. Many people, dressed similarly to her detail, gave the same impression of being invisible. A man and woman to her left watched an interaction beyond her line of sight. Riesman sighed.

What's the FBI doing here?

Unable to see what they were observing, Riesman reined in her wandering mind and focused on her feet. The wet grass was difficult to navigate, and the warm weather out of place for November in Cambridge, Massachusetts. With every step closer to the casket, her heart slowed and her breath shortened, as if an elephant was sitting on her chest. Riesman tried to shift her thoughts to the climate, to work, to anything but Hiaki and his family just ahead.

Hiaki's smiling face with his caring eyes appeared in front of her. *Why did you leave? Years of super storms, flooding in the mid-west and Texas, volcanic activity in the Pacific Rim, melting polar caps ... we were supposed to find the answers ... something to do with miscalculating the planets' orbits. Hiaki. Why?* She blinked her eyes, his face melted away, and she realized that she was shaking Hiaki's grieving widow's hand.

"I am so sorry for your loss, Dr. Nakamura. Your husband was a great scientist," Riesman said, unable to look her in the eye, and grateful that her dark glasses hid her shame. The widow's grip surprised her.

Mrs. Nakamura gave Riesman a forced smile, then her eyes drifted to the casket. "Thank you so much, Dr. Riesman, for coming today. Hiaki spoke very highly of you. He was fortunate to have a boss and friend like you for so many years." The widow continued to hold her hand and gaze at the casket.

Riesman's mouth tightened and more tears brimmed in her eyes.

Oh God! Please help me!

Unable to say anything or to escape the woman's grip, Riesman's desperation built and her knees grew weaker by the second.

Mrs. Nakamura finally released her hand and looked at her. "I know you can only stay for a short time, so I put you near the back of the luncheon with some former co-workers. I hope you don't mind." The widow's deep, brown tear-filled eyes swallowed Riesman up.

She fought the urge to flee and forced herself to smile, nod and then repeat the same sentence to everyone else down the family line: "I am so sorry for your loss. Please accept my condolences."

It was the longest three minutes she'd experienced in some time. Her mind was running wild, trying to find some excuse to avoid going to the luncheon, when she caught sight of an older, light-skinned Hispanic man who looked familiar. He stood in the distance engaged in an intense conversation with a well-dressed, regal-looking man. A young woman who might have been his granddaughter stood beside him and held the man's arm.

Riesman moved onto the road to obtain a better vantage point and noticed the two FBI agents watching the men as well. After a moment, she remembered why the man looked so familiar, and had he not been engaged in an argument, she would've run over and given him a huge hug. Suddenly, the couple left. The Hispanic man called after them in a tone laced with hostility—unusual for him from what she remembered.

"We're not done here, *Sir* Pierce." He made the sarcasm quite clear.

Riesman slowed her pace until she was sure she had accurately identified him. *No way! It's impossible!* She stopped around eight feet away and stared at him while others worked their way around her. Other than the FBI, no one else had noticed the hostile interaction.

"Do you know him, ma'am?" her driver asked.

"Yeah. As I live and breathe, I know him," she replied, pleasantly surprised by the chance meeting. She picked up her pace again and stopped before him. It took him a moment to realize who she was, then his anger evaporated, he smiled, and she embraced her old friend.

"Captain Anthony Perez! I never thought I would find you here! How are you, old man?" She pulled back to take a better look, surprised at how fit he looked for his age. His arms, chest, and back felt as if they were made of stone. Even his face and neck had the chiseled look of a young man.

"It's been a long time, Bobbie Jo." In a matter of seconds, her old friend's therapeutic voice eased her feelings of emptiness and guilt. She stepped out of his embrace and took him all in—black suit and tie, crisp white shirts, very short black cropped hair with only small patches of white betraying his age.

"Whatever you're doing, I need to get some. I saw you over twenty years ago ..."

"Twenty-three years, but who's counting? I've been lucky with good genes and time for exercising."

"And writing too, I hear."

"One published book does not an author make," he said sheepishly. "Kind of the right thing, in the right place at the right time."

"I bet sales went through the roof when the New York Times called your work uplifting, enlightening, and thought provoking," Riesman teased.

He nodded and looked down while he walked, his hands thrust into the pockets of his buttoned suit jacket. Even his voice sounded stronger than she remembered. "That book is about fifteen years old and it was unusually successful. It allowed me an opportunity to forge ahead with a small practice and teaching. Still, you're right. I did find some time per day to exercise, and I eat pretty well."

"Well, it's great to see you in spite of the circumstances." A sudden onslaught of emotions threatened to consume her, so she tried to find more questions to avoid her sadness. Unfortunately, she stalled as she remembered that Perez's son and wife had been killed in a tragic car accident nearly twenty years ago when he dropped off the map. She thought he had a daughter but was afraid to ask. When his book came out, she'd found the courage to call him. He'd been gracious and kind, but graver than before.

"So, did you know Dr. Nakamura through work?" he asked, just as she was about to ask him the same question.

"Yes. He worked on my team. And how about you?" she asked quickly. *Breathe, Roberta. Just breathe.*

"I worked with his wife several years back. A family matter on her side."

Riesman glanced at him. Out of the thousands of discussions in the office, over dinner and breakfast, or in the bedroom, nothing registered about any family member having a mental health issue.

"Are you going to the luncheon? I plan on staying very briefly myself," he asked.

Her driver held her car door open. She still couldn't think of an excuse not to go, but her final answer surprised her. "Yes."

Perez smiled before walking away. "I'll see you there, Bobbie Jo."

She watched him go, noting his determined yet relaxed gait and square backside. Though more than two decades had passed since they'd worked together at the Veterans' Administration Hospital, she didn't remember him being so solidly built. The two FBI agents followed him at a distance. While baffled as to why they were following her former boss, his physical appearance struck her as even stranger.

He's got to be sixty or more. How can he look like he's thirty? I should read his book.

Peter's voice brought her back. "Are we going to the luncheon, ma'am?"

"Yes," she replied as she got into the car. "Have Diane look at my afternoon schedule, too."

"Yes, ma'am."

After adjusting her nylons, she shed her jacket, wiped her shoes on the car mat, and noted with pleasure that her driver already had the air-conditioning on. Tablets, papers, and folders full of unfinished work spilled from her open brief case and spread across the seat. Now she had one more anomaly to figure out. What was Perez doing here?

Riesman pulled her mirror, eyeliner and lipstick out of her handbag. After a few minutes of applying makeup, she stopped. "When you age, you're supposed to look older, right?"

~

November 14, 2023 A.D. - Two hours later

"I gather you're not a fan of the man and woman you were talking to?" Riesman took the last bite of her garlic mash potatoes.

"Sir Robert Philip Pierce," Perez said with contempt. "He's a traitor and a miscreant; too good to be so, and too bad to live." He looked out the restaurant's window.

Riesman's eyes widened. Several times during their conversation he'd sounded as if he were reading from a classic book when a simple yes or no would have sufficed. She'd held onto his every word despite the noise of people talking, his quoting, and the three glasses of wine. She picked up her second cup of coffee and blew on it.

"What? He's a miscreant?"

Perez's eyes shone as he slipped into his old teaching mode. "Sorry, Bobbie Jo, but I have a history with this guy. And I wish I could say I composed that saying, but William Shakespeare got to it first. I think it was one of the Richards plays, maybe *Richard II*. I'd rather talk about anything but that sack of crap."

"Okay. Then tell me how come you look twenty years younger?"

She'd taken two gulps of coffee before it looked as if he might respond; a surprising length of time to answer what she thought was a simple question. "What is it? Steroids or something?"

"Nope. I eliminated all processed foods and I've focused on exercise."

Since nothing more followed, Riesman leaned forward and extended her hands, palms up, as if asking, 'Well?'

"No. That's it. Really. I wish there was more."

"There's more, but you're not saying it. Come on, Anthony— I was born at night, but it wasn't last night."

"Do you remember our ward unit's psychologist? She was Indian and always messed up phrases like that. You know, she would say something like, I was born at night, but it was yesterday. Now what was her name ...?"

"Stop, Anthony! You're stalling and doing a piss poor job at it too," Riesman said. "Usually, I'm not so vain, but I'm in my mid-forties, and I'm killing myself to stay healthy and looking young. Yes, I said it: looking young. But you look younger than I remember twenty years ago. Not to be biased, and I may be projecting, but for a guy who has to be in his sixties, I would have mistaken you for late thirties."

"Just thirty?"

Riesman put down her coffee, folded her arms, and waited.

"Did I mention that I spend about three hours a day exercising?" he said.

"No way! There is no way you can convince me that exercising every day and eating nothing but natural, unprocessed food has halted your aging, or rather reversed your aging in your case. It's not my first day on the job, Anthony. I'm not that young, impressionable trainee who's just showed up on the admissions' unit, accepting without questioning your word as gospel." Riesman spoke a little louder than she wanted to. Fortunately, the noise level from the full restaurant covered it.

Okay. Less wine and more coffee, she thought and lifted her cup.

"Yeah ... she was funny," he said.

"Who?"

"The unit director. I said, the only easy day was yesterday, and she'd mess it up later and say, the only hard day is tomorrow."

Riesman put down her coffee and looked at him. "Are you done?"

"Ah yes, the old days of me telling you to just do it are forever gone. You never did strike me as the kind of woman who'd just follow orders. It's a good quality, you know," he said.

A waiter appeared with a thermos of fresh coffee. He refreshed her coffee and took her dinner plate away. Perez waved off an offer of coffee. Riesman noticed that his drinks and appetizers remained untouched, and he'd only picked at his food.

"I would never expect the Executive Director of Readiness and Disaster Logistics in FEMA's Office of Response and Recovery to accept at face value any statement so fantastic without the required data and analysis to support it," he continued.

Riesman sipped her hot coffee and observed him closely. He looked out the window. The thought that her former boss and mentor knew her present position, role, and title at the Federal Emergency Management Agency made her uncomfortable. How could he know that when they'd assigned her new title just three week ago with an internal memorandum? It hadn't appeared on the organizational chart.

Rather than ask another question, Riesman pulled a clinical strategy from her mentor's own treatment strategies and said nothing. The din from the luncheon guests rose, and he too remained silent for a few moments. Then he smiled even more. Clearly, he'd picked up that she waited for some kind of response. Whether deliberate or not, Perez did go on, but not in the expected direction.

"Flour, sugar, chemicals, all that stuff I cut out fifteen years ago. High intensity exercise, especially weight bearing, in combination with eating non-processed food, has made a profound difference. Add to that teaching, helping people, and biblio-therapy, I can truly say that the stress in my life has dropped off to nothing."

"Biblio-therapy? So you've discovered another treatment strategy?"

"No, Bobbie Jo. I wish. Biblio-therapy is another way of saying I've been writing. Freud was the one who discovered the art of writing down a stream of unconscious to get at neurosis, traumas and such. In other words, it helps when I write."

"Speaking of writing, I did see that your book, while highly regarded, was quite short." *Darn! I jumped to another subject. There was more. Man, my clinical skills have rusted.*

"Eighty-two pages. Long enough to get my point across, and short enough for people to actually read it without skimming and scanning."

"Well, it did work well, and it was inspirational. How did you come up with your title ... what was it?" Riesman stopped with her coffee half way to her lips.

"*Life's Directives: Twenty Ways to Live a Healthy Life.*" He picked up his phone.

Two things struck Riesman at the same time: first, his expression had become remote and dark at the mention of his book, and the size of his smart phone was larger than any she'd seen before. Too big for a smart phone, it had to be a tablet.

"When my daughter died and I was left alone, I had a choice to make, live or die. As simple as it sounds, I needed a reason to live. After a great deal of soul searching and looking at everything possible, I found some inspirational Roman artifacts, and they became the impetus for writing my book," he said in a matter-of-fact tone as he looked at the tablet.

The news of his daughter's death stunned Riesman. How could all that happen to one guy? And how had she missed such a tragedy? Her friend's entire family had gone, and she felt ashamed that this was the first she'd heard of it. Guilt, sadness, and anger at herself swept over her leaving her sad and empty. How could a man who lost both his children and a wife, albeit more than fifteen years ago, appear so serene and focused? Could she ever achieve the same level of equanimity?

Living without Hiaki was going to be unbearable. She glanced at Hiaki's wife and daughters—a life she would never have. She shook herself out of her despair and turned back to her old mentor. Perez was touching his screen. After a moment, he tucked it back in his pocket with one hand and placed his napkin on the table with his other, then stood without a word.

Peter's sudden appearance startled her. "Director? Administrator Damon needs to speak with you. It's urgent," he whispered in her ear.

Riesman frowned. With the number of directors in the chain of command between her and the administrator, why would he contact her? What disaster could have happened for him to call her directly? She stood, anxiety rising, and turned to excuse herself, but Perez embraced her in a hug.

"Looks like duty calls us both. If you're not doing anything next week and find yourself in Massachusetts, come on over for Thanksgiving. I'm having a couple of colleagues over for dinner, dance, and fun. No pressure. Just if you're around."

Her anxiety shifted to curiosity. She nodded but wondered how Perez knew that work had called. He might have guessed, but it could have been a family emergency.

"Ma'am? We have to go," Peter said.

Perez's firm grip fell away. He smiled and turned to leave before she could respond.

"Hope to see you soon, Bobbie Jo," he said without looking back. A sudden urge to ask for more details almost set her after him. He'd disappeared through the exit already, and by the time she made it to the veranda, he was getting into the back seat of a large, high-end green sedan with tinted windows that obscured the occupants. The car moved as his door closed and drove out of sight.

"Is everything all right, Ma'am?" Peter asked.

"Yes ... everything's all right," she replied, but she couldn't help feeling as if something was completely wrong.

~

November 14, 2023 A.D. - Five hours later

There's absolutely no sound in this office, Riesman thought. She sat on a leather couch, staring at a large plasma television embedded in the mahogany paneled wall in front of her. Closed captions flowed in large print beneath continuous images of the national and international news. The pair of smaller monitors flanking it showed local coverage of disasters occurring around the US.

She could see why Administrator Damon never had to visit any disaster areas, unless it was at the White House. Riesman stood to shake the cramps from her legs and, for the third time, walked the perimeter of the office and examined the dozens of presidential citations and congressional awards. Then she listed all the ways her ten by ten office with its generic faux wood and plastic veneer differed from his thirty by thirty foot office with its polished pen holders, heavy oak furniture and matching rugs and drapes.

She still wore her black funeral attire and had the smell of old, dry coffee on her breath. An escort had whisked her off to the Administrator's office as soon as the private jet landed, and the male secretary had brought her straight into the office, so she'd had no time to reapply her makeup and freshen up. While brusque, the secretary was kind enough to bring cups, a thermos of coffee, and a message that she would need to wait some time until he arrived.

The time would've passed quickly if her smart phone had worked in the office. The only time she'd stepped out of the office was to get a signal.

"Your phone is not rated or equipped to penetrate the signal dampening fields," the secretary had said. "You also don't have clearance to use any phones here. I am sorry, but could you please return to the office?"

He hadn't sounded sorry. Riesman had returned to her seat and fumed about all the mystery and the time she was wasting. She also thought about her interaction with Perez and the bureau's clampdown on Hiaki's computer.

And why is there a dampening field in this office? A new protocol?

A caption caught her eye on the main news channel. General David Farrell, in full uniform, was giving an interview. Riesman returned to her seat, picked up her cup of coffee, and resumed reading the captions. Farrell, a man of mystery with an even more mysterious series of projects, all associated with space, was very high up in the Pentagon and never gave interviews. He sat calm and at ease with his hands folded on his lap, shoulders rounded, and face relaxed.

Interviewer: " ...you haven't denied the existence of another celestial body affecting our orbit. That said, do you acknowledge that there is something out there?"

Farrell: "I can't confirm or deny what's out there. But what I can say is that we're eighteen months away from launching a series of manned exploration missions, including two to Mars."

Interviewer: "So you're not willing to confirm or deny Planet X's existence, but at the same time, American tax dollars will fund a mission for something you're not willing to say is real?"

Farrell: "I think I just said that. But let me say it another way. Whether there is or is not a Planet X, we will soon find out. If no Planet X exists, we still have a problem as to why our orbit is slightly off kilter. If there is a hidden planet, then we have our answer and life goes on."

Interviewer: "But how would it be possible not to see it? We've had spacecraft of all sorts out there. You'd think we'd have seen it by now."

Farrell: "Yup. You'd think that ..."

"Good evening, Ms. Riesman."

She jumped at the Administrator's voice, spilling some of her coffee on herself, the couch, and the rug. As usual, Administrator Richard Damon had arrived with two other people, a younger man and woman, right behind him. All three wore the same dark suit, shirt and similar accessories. The man and woman weren't the same two people she'd seen at the funeral, but they looked similar.

Riesman put her cup down and stood to shake his hand. "Good evening, Administrator."

"Good evening." He walked to his seat, reading on a tablet.

She retracted her unshaken hand and took a seat closer to his desk. The Administrator introduced the other two people without looking up from his tablet.

This is one the most bizarre and rude situations I've been in for a long time.

"These are Special Agents Arthur Harper and Donna Lee. They're helping us with our internal investigations," Damon said.

Internal investigations? On who?

"They've been working on the Nakamura and Perez case for years."

Riesman's heart jumped and her breath came up short at the mention of Hiaki Nakamura, Anthony Perez and internal investigation all in the same breath. Riesman wished she had better control over her emotions; she'd be terrible at covert operations.

"What? Why is Hiaki under investigation, and what does Anthony have to do with him, or anything?"

Damon looked up from his tablet and stared at Riesman. Her emotions had apparently taken him by surprise. Though embarrassed by her own reaction, she maintained the eye contact, not in the mood to back down.

"Agent Harper? Agent Lee? Bring the director up to speed, please," he said as he broke eye contact and returned to reading.

Agent Harper was a handsome young man with well-manicured hands, a warm smile and just a hint of musk and sensuality—a candidate for dating had she been fifteen years younger. He approached with a tablet and held it in front of her. "Director? Do you know this woman?"

Riesman looked at the image of a serious looking young woman, maybe in her early twenties, surrounded by computers and white boards filled with all kinds of equations. Her mocha skin color, blue eyes and long curly hair made a striking and familiar picture, but no name popped into her head. "She looks familiar, but I don't have a name."

"Her name is Doctor Andrea Perez," Lee said.

Riesman looked again. The woman had a different eye color and lighter skin but the same shaped face, jaw line and eyes as her father, Anthony Perez.

"This has to be years ago. He told me that she died …"

"Who told you that?" Agent Lee asked.

Riesman sized her up: handsome and well put together like Agent Harper, but less familiar and kind. She looked back at the picture as she formulated her answer. "Anthony Perez told me this no more than six hours ago. We attended the funeral and luncheon of Dr. Hiaki Nakamura earlier this morning."

"We know you were there, Director," Harper said.

"This picture was taken about fifteen years ago," Lee said. "Dr. Perez was a brilliant scientist in the area of spectrograph analysis and light, and how they might be bent or manipulated. She was on the cusp of rewriting some key equations that would have changed the way we think of light."

"Dr. Perez had taken the mathematical works of Newton, Einstein, Hawking, Guth … all of them, and produced a series of formulas that would not only change our understanding of the world but also give us the right tools, calibrated the right way, so we could see things that we couldn't before," Harper added.

Riesman frowned. *Things we couldn't see before?*

"Like when the *Hubble's* lens was repaired. The entire universe opened up," Lee said.

"Okay. But she's gone, right? And what does it have to do with Dr. Nakamura? He was a mathematician and statistician in light and wavelengths."

Her mind bounced back and forth between Perez, his daughter and Nakamura. The confusing new data was too personal and close to her heart.

"Dr. Perez was not into astronomy either, and she's not dead," Lee replied. "Missing? Yes—she's been missing for the last fifteen years. And her connection with Dr. Nakamura—he continued her work. He made progress where everyone else had failed."

Riesman's balance wavered as she tried to process all the information at once. Harper produced another image. This time of her beloved Hiaki sitting on a park bench with Anthony Perez right beside him. Both men looked very serious, as if they held the world on their shoulders. Riesman reached out to touch the tablet, but Harper pulled it away.

"This picture was taken three months ago when you and Dr. Nakamura were staying at the Queen Anne Hotel in Montreal," he said.

Riesman's gaze dropped to the floor, her face and neck flushed with heat. She thought her pale Wyoming skin and blonde hair must have looked like a genetically altered Maine lobster with white limbs and hair. "How long have you known?" It took all her courage to look at the Administrator. He stared at her—unlike the first part of the meeting.

"Probably right from the beginning, five years ago, but that's not important," Lee replied. "What is important is that Mr. Perez was in contact with Dr. Nakamura three months before he died. His daughter went missing while working on a contract with NASA and the Department of Defense. And Mr. Perez tells you that she's dead. We have looked everywhere for her. It's as if she's fallen off the planet. And, after all of these coincidences and mysteries, Mr. Perez shows up at Dr. Nakamura's private funeral, specifically arranged by us and kept out of the paper, internet and everything. Mr. Perez is in the center of a great deal of mysteries." He laced the last line with a dose of sarcasm.

"Then why don't you bring him in?"

"Because Perez is not who we want. We want his sponsor, Ms. Christine Reich."

Riesman, frowning in confusion, glanced from Harper to Lee and settled on Damon. "What? Do you mean *the* Christine Reich? No one's ever seen her. She's a ghost. And how is Anthony connected to Reich?"

"We're not sure. But Andrea Perez's work had another sponsor, Reich Enterprise's telecommunications branch, along with NASA and DOD. Again, it was there that she was on the cusp of something great, and then she disappeared, along with every piece of her work. Reich's officials blamed corporate espionage, but her lab, computers and home were so thoroughly destroyed that it's hard to really believe that an outside corporation had anything to do with it. We won't bring Perez in unless we are sure he's connected to Reich and get some leverage on him," Harper explained.

"And that leverage is you, Director Riesman," Lee said. "He did ask you to join him for Thanksgiving, right? He said there would be some friends there." The question was rhetorical.

Riesman focused on Damon. Dry sweat stuck to her clothes, and a chill ran down her back. Processing the information had drained her, but she managed to pull some moisture into her mouth and croak out some words. "You … want me to spy on Anthony and his guests at Thanksgiving?"

Exposed and confused, Riesman waited for Damon to respond to her directly. Based on everything that had transpired in the past twelve hours, it must have been evident that she wanted some answers. It took Administrator Damon a moment to answer, albeit carefully and slowly.

"Roberta, Drs. Perez and Nakamura were the best minds this country had ever developed. We as a government and as a country invested time, money, resources and access to classified data so they could advance the human race. And just when the deliverables are within reach, they disappear and die. Behind all of this is one woman—a German national, private industrialist and financier, Christine Reich. A woman of multiple talents, heavily resourced and thought to be the wealthiest woman in the world. And yet the world's best intelligence agencies can't even get a picture of her, nor can we find any record of her past, school, church, parking violations, nothing. Now we have an opportunity to connect all the players. And you are the one person he seems to trust. If we have an opportunity to get them all together, including even a chance of meeting this mystery woman Reich, then the answer is yes, you will be spying next Thursday on Thanksgiving. It will be for flag and country. But if it helps, we are not interested in Perez, just his guests and some answers."

It took a moment, but Riesman nodded as if she acquiesced. Her thoughts and heart were still with Hiaki—his warm smile and soft eyes. "All right." Judging by the quick looks they exchanged, her answer had taken them by surprise.

"All right then, Director Riesman. I assume you know this is classified at the highest levels and is not to be shared with anyone outside of this room," Agent Harper said.

"Yes."

"We will be in contact with you, starting on Monday, to go over questions and fit you with wires for tracking and listening," Lee said.

"Yes." The room remained silent then, so she stood with her bag, nodded and waited to be dismissed.

"You know your way out, Roberta," Damon said.

"Thank you."

Riesman turned and walked slowly to the door. She noted, as she passed through the administrative assistant's office, that the assistant was also elegantly dressed and manicured. After leaving the antechamber, she walked in silence down the series of hallways, mechanically producing her badge, bag and herself for inspection at the several checkpoints throughout the Homeland Security building. Fifteen minutes later, she sat in the back seat of her car, with a different driver and protection team, all of them immaculately dressed with similar accessories and manicured hands. Riesman looked out the window with multiple thoughts running through her head. Every time she rewound the conversation, she got stuck on the same couple of things.

Why is the Department of Defense involved? A weapon? What does Hiaki and Anthony have to do with all this?

Chapter Five

WHAT'S HAPPENED TO YOU? *You're not this man. I don't know this guy.* Riesman stared at the primitive artifacts scattered on Perez's walls and tables. She moved closer to the mounted spears, easily seven feet long with heavy-looking metal tips and different colored feathers at the other end. The level of detail was impressive. After close inspection of other edged weapons, Riesman stopped and really looked around. Various flowers in pots attached to large columns gave the only hint of life in the spartan living room. Paleolithic era weapons and shields hung on every wall, interspersed with, and in stark contrast to, the abstract art scattered throughout the apartment. Expansive floor-to-ceiling windows overlooked the Boston Gardens, and the strong smells of honey, cinnamon and lilac filled the air. Rock and roll played too loud for her liking.

"It's another world."

Perez and his three other guests worked as a team, laughing and chatting in German while they cleaned and put away the Thanksgiving dinner plates. All three were short women with varying shades and length of red hair, and all three wore loose-fitting turtle-neck blouses over black tights. They gyrated to the music as they worked.

Riesman sipped the wine she'd brought as a gift along with a purchased, baked apple pie. She still had no idea why Perez was with them. Money, not looks, was her clinical analysis; roommates for the expensive piece of real estate—a penthouse in Boston proper.

Riesman looked out the grand windows. The building lights flickered on as the city skyline darkened.

She sipped more of her second glass of expensive wine, uncomfortable both with her task as a spy and where Agent Lee had put the tracking/transceiver device. Riesman walked around, hoping that both gravity and Kegel moves might help, but she only made it worse. She took another sip and tried to distract herself by analyzing the three women.

With red hair and large, dark eyes, they didn't fit the German stereotype of the tall, blonde, blue-eyed Aryan. They had the robust quality though. Uniformly five feet in height, they had a broad, square build with muscular legs and arms. Riesman tried to look closely without being rude. Their facial features were not very feminine. All three had sloping foreheads, broad faces, broader jaws, and expansive eyes, set back and well protected by their brows. If it wasn't for their hair, they'd have quite an exposed overhang, Riesman thought. Images of *Neanderthal* humans came to mind.

I gotta say that for chicks who are pretty homely, they sure act like they're the hot models around town. You gotta respect that.

Riesman smiled and sipped her wine, glad that she fell well within the American ideal. Feeling suddenly self-conscious of her own appearance, she smoothed out her elegant, midnight-blue pencil dress and chided herself for being catty and shallow.

The women, still dancing to the music, placed desserts, tea and coffee on the table while Perez finished cleaning the kitchen. The setting and people were so surreal that she found herself forgetting why she was really there. The transceiver's location reminded her. She walked around the room again. It still didn't help.

Who are you, Anthony? Was it the loss of your entire family that changed you into who you are now, whatever that is? Are you in some cult? What happened to that simple, overweight, gregarious guy?

She realized she was staring at Perez. He fiddled with his small tablet—or was it a large phone?—clearly immersed in something. He'd never struck her as a technophile, but he'd never been far from his tablet all night, and it was the oddest one she'd ever seen: very sleek lines, no ports, almost like a smooth piece of marble. When its screen was off, it looked like polished stone.

Her gaze wandered to the set of primitive weapons that hung on the wall above his head, then to the martial statues on the table beside him. When she refocused on him, he was nodding and talking quietly to himself or his tablet. He made eye contact and walked over.

"I'm sorry for the delay, Bobbie Jo. Are you ready for dessert?" he asked.

Riesman pointed to his tablet. "I've never seen a tablet like that. Can I take a look?"

He raised an eyebrow and blinked, as if taking a moment to understand what she was asking. A strange look crossed his face, then he smiled and handed her the tablet while offering to take her wine with his other hand. "It's a little heavier than it looks."

She exchanged her wine for the tablet. It did feel heavier than she expected, and unlike a regular tablet or smart phone, had no visible buttons, slides, or controls. Both sides looked and felt like a polished, flat stone—perhaps light marble or granite. She'd never seen anything like it before. She turned the phone over again, looking for the screen housing.

"The screen is on the other side and is activated by you looking at it."

"Oh? That's pretty high tech for a therapist like you."

Riesman looked at the stone, and a low, green light began to pulsate slowly. She held it firmly in both hands, and warmth flowed through her fingers, but the rich green light intrigued her more. The more she looked, the deeper into the depths of the object it drew her. The light grew, and her fingertips heated further, but it aroused curiosity and puzzlement, not alarm. A vivid sensation came over her of a dark, warm, protected cavity, then a constriction followed by a rush of cold air that embraced her whole body. A cough, a sharp slap on her buttocks, then an image of her mother's beautiful blue eyes looking down on her.

Mum? You're so young ...

More images and sensations flew by. She saw herself as a little girl entering kindergarten, falling off her bicycle and being picked up her father and sister in third grade, the strong smell of cow manure, and the rush of riding her favorite horse. She saw herself delivering her first calf on the farm, followed by driving her family's tractor in the corn field on a brutally hot day. She saw and felt the neighbor boy's very first kiss. Middle and high school flashed through her mind, as did her first orgasm. Cold days, hot nights, and warm beer came and went, as did visions of her first day in officer training; all the ways to a firefight in Iran. The flashes came faster, and so did the days and nights of her past: some tender visions, others of dead friends and soldiers. She felt intensely throughout the experience: happiness, pain, tenderness, fear and sorrow. A vivid image of meeting Perez arose, and one of her running her first clinical group, followed by completing her doctorate and explaining to her parents why she was not moving back to Wyoming.

More visions came—various assignments, friends and lovers—and only slowed at her appointment to FEMA and the news of Perez's family tragedy. They sped up again with tense, sad moments at her mother and father's funeral, and she watched her nieces and nephews grow before her eyes. The visions slowed again at her last lovemaking with Hiaki, attending his funeral, lunch with Perez, her meeting with the Administrator and agents.

Finally, she saw Agent Lee making sure that the audio devices and internal tracking system was as comfortable as any large tampon.

Riesman shook her head. The green light blazed brighter. Her hands shot to her eyes, and the tablet clattered onto the floor. Her knees weakened, but Perez's strong arms caught her before she fell.

"I got you."

She rubbed her eyes and blinked. It worked well. Her vision cleared quickly and the heat subsided from her fingers.

"What the hell was that, Perez? Thanks for the warning ... Does ... does it always do that?" It took her a moment longer to regain her balance, sight and wits.

"Only sometimes," Perez replied. "It can give me a nasty static shock on dry days like this." He checked that she could stand alone, then stepped away.

Static shock? Are you kidding me? It was something much more than that.

Perez picked up the tablet and looked at it briefly. Surprisingly, the glossy surface displayed no finger prints, and no dents or damage from its drop to the hard marble floor.

"I'm sorry, Bobbie Jo. The tablet also has a biochemical defense mechanism. I thought I'd turned it off, but by your response, I expect you experienced a series of emotionally powerful images, important ones, I bet?"

"Are you kidding me? It's like I experienced my entire life's highlights in seconds. So if someone unauthorized holds it they get a here's-your-life show while you tackle him? You're kidding me, right? Wouldn't a biochemical knock-out zap be easier?"

She tried to make light of the event, but when she rewound the moments just prior to holding the tablet, she remembered how Perez had put her drink down to free both hands, almost in preparation to use them if necessary.

She concluded that it wasn't a mistake. She glanced beyond him to the three women. They looked at her with stunned expressions.

Riesman took the glass of wine back, glad that she didn't make a total spectacle of herself.

"*Um Himmels willen, Terra und Erde! Die blonde Gigantin hat eine Verwandtschaft zu unserem Stamm. Das hätte ich nie erwartet,*" one of the women said in a surprised tone.

Great! Here comes the German again.

"*Einverstanden! Wieso ist sie so groß geworden, nachdem sie so viel verarbeitetes Mehl und Getreide gegessen hat? Denk nur, was passieren würde, wenn sie sich gesund ernähren würde! Denkst du, daß die Gigantin noch größer wäre?*" the other woman asked.

"You know, Anthony, this speaking German is getting pretty old," Riesman complained. Perez rolled his eyes at the women's exchange as if he understood them. The pygmy women had spoken German all through their time together. They spoke English occasionally, but only to ask her to move or tell her where to sit. This exchange had been the most she'd heard from them, and she was sure they were talking about her.

"*Sie kann kein Deutsch, meine Damen. Seien wir nicht unhöflich,*" he said as he led her to her chair at the table.

Riesman shot a look at Perez. She'd never heard him speak another language other than Spanish, and even that was rare. *German! You speak German? You live in a Boston penthouse with three women, walls covered in primitive art, and you speak fluent German. Who the hell are you?*

"*Unglaublich! Sie kann die Sprache ihres Stammes doch überhaupt nicht? Armes Ding, siehst du, Milites Lux und Vespere? Sie hat ihre Vorfahren, ihre Abstammung vergessen und sie tötet sich langsam durch ihre Ernährung. Ich wette, sie möchte lieber in der Sonne liegen als sich zu verstecken und sich von UV-Strahlen zu schützen. Armes Ding. Und sie hat noch mindestens acht Prozent des genetischen Codes unserer Erbschaft? Erstaunlich!*" Dee Dee said in a tone of contained enthusiasm as they sat down for dessert.

"Please," Perez said with a look as he took his own seat.

"Sorry, Immunes, I will focus. I thought Riesman knew German because of her last name. I apologize, Riesman," Dee Dee said in perfect, though heavily accented, English.

For a moment, Riesman found herself unable to respond or move. She couldn't tell if the reason was the experience with the tablet, the revelation that at least one of the women spoke English and Perez spoke German, or the use of certain words such as 'immunes.'

Does that mean she heard my pygmy comment earlier? Shit!

Riesman replayed when she'd said it, her volume, and where everyone was at the time. She tried to push down the embarrassment and focus on something else. Perez dipped his spoon into some earth-colored, graham-cracker-textured dessert. She tore her eyes from the vile plate, and tried to repeat the word she hadn't understood.

"Immunes is a title from Latin that means something like a specialized soldier, such as Special Forces."

"Latin? As in dead language?"

"Yup. Roman Empire, Tacitus, Cicero, Caesar. Oldies but goodies."

"And it means specialized forces like a Delta squad?"

"Delta, Omega and Epsilon. All trained for specialized missions. That's what immunes means. Kind of cool, huh?"

"*Epsilon* Team? Really? An all *woman* 'Delta Force?' That's just a myth; some Navy SEAL guy's fantasy."

"Maybe not here, but other governments might have such a force."

Riesman was about to continue when she noticed that she was the only one having a piece of the apple pie. Perez took a tiny sliver—a no-thank-you-but-I'm-not-interested-in-this-food size her mother had trained her to take when confronted with offensive food. To her surprise, he'd taken a larger helping of the dirt-like substance the other women ate so eagerly. The large quantity of food the women ate amazed her. The Thanksgiving meal had been composed of protein rich meats and fowls of all sorts, followed by legumes and vegetables—no starches to speak of. She'd asked one of the women about the drinks and learned that they contained no alcohol but lots of blueberry and blackberry juice. It tasted more like pure extract than a sugared drink. The women also used large thick bowls for their dessert; similar to what they'd used at dinner. Riesman sighed and tried to figure out why she was getting very angry.

"So does anyone else want some pie I …"

All three women said no before she could get the last syllable of her question out, as if she'd offered them poison. Worse, they pulled their own dessert closer as if she might take it. As if she wanted that pile of dirt!

"What are you eating?" she asked in an attempt to contain her surprise and rising anger.

The women frowned and looked at each other as if trying to figure out what she was saying. Again, Dee Dee spoke for them all. "Why, it's baked chestnuts with crushed almonds, and coconut soaked in its own juices with cinnamon and lemon topping."

Riesman's jaw slackened. At first, she thought the woman must be joking, but the other two women returned to eating their treat with gusto.

My God! What have I've fallen into here?

Riesman put her fork down and looked around the table. She was not used to being the odd one out, or being ignored or avoided. Her jaw clenched and her heart rate rose. She picked up her wine glass, swirled the contents for a moment, and then, frustrated, plonked it down with more force than necessary. Thud. The others turned their heads at the sound. She closed her eyes and organized her thoughts.

"What is your problem with me? Why would you speak German when clearly I'm an American, and you can obviously speak the language?"

"*Est-ce que la géante préférait-elle le français?*" Vespere asked.

"*Non ...je ne pense pas qu'elle puisse parler français non plus. Pourquoi ces gens ne peuvent pas apprendre les langues de leur monde?*" Lux said to Vespere.

"What! What is that? French? Now you're speaking French?" Riesman's voice rose.

"Ladies! That's enough! Stop badgering her. She's a guest and that's discourteous," Perez said, then he turned to Dee Dee.

"Milites Vespere and Lux! Silence!" she said with authority to the other women.

Silence filled the room. Riesman looked at all of them before turning to Perez. He sat quietly with his elbows on the table, hands folded beneath his chin, looking down at the table.

"Anthony, what the hell is going on here? This isn't you. You lived in the suburbs and had ... normal friends. These women don't belong here. You don't belong here with them, in this apartment. You couldn't have changed that much. I know you had losses ..." Sadness filled her heart at the thought of her own loss; Hiaki dying, gone forever. She would have continued, but Perez's head snapped up when she mentioned his loss. He sat back and glared. Riesman blinked; never before had he directed anger at her.

His eyes narrowed, jaw line tightened and he placed his hands on the table. "And you know my pain, Bobbie Jo?"

The kind, gentle soul she thought she knew dissolved in front of her, leaving a hardened effigy. He stared through her for a moment, then looked at his hands and uneaten dessert. Riesman wanted to reach out, but he looked up again, less hard and more of the person she had known for years, but still different.

"There are some things that are bigger than us. Things greater in scale and scope that dwarf our own problems, tragedies, hopes and dreams. Visions of the future can only be fully grasped if we look beyond ourselves and see that we are only part of a larger plan, a small cog in a machine."

"What do you mean?"

"I mean bigger truths that once known will shake the very core of our existence," Perez continued. "While our own planet sits on the very doorstep of its own demise, it's not the biggest problem to humanity. Deadly, dangerous, extinction level events bubble just under the surface of the planet's crust, and they're the least of our worries. The biggest narcissistic injury is yet to come. There are only a few people, very few, who can prepare our government that will in turn prepare a nation and world for the biggest existential answer to a long-standing question: are we alone? We've never been alone. The one who knows this carries great despair and responsibility to act outside the norms, beyond the laws and above all else, to teach a race of people not to strike out in fear and anger but to sit back and learn. So different is this from our nature. We attack what we don't know. It takes a special type of person to lead the way and convince a planet to save itself and its soul. This is big, even bigger than my personal loss." Perez fell silent and looked through the windows to the Boston skyline.

Riesman stared at him, unable to understand his words or look away from the man and the dark abyss into which he fell. She wondered if he were crazy. She wanted to say something reassuring and comforting but couldn't think of anything that could counter his eloquent tirade.

The younger woman, Lux, caught her off guard when she spoke clearly in a thickly accented, low tone but in perfect English. "…'His very existence was improbable, inexplicable, and altogether bewildering. He was an insoluble problem. It was inconceivable how he had existed, how he had succeeded in getting so far, how he had managed to remain—why he did not instantly disappear.'"

Riesman's mouth slackened, and she stared at the woman, stunned by her ability to verbalize her own thoughts, truly capturing the moment.

Vespere, who nodded as if she approved of the statement, answered an unasked question. "J. Conrad's work, *Heart of Darkness and the Congo Diary*. A fine choice, Lux. I was thinking more J. Milton's *Paradise Lost* quote of 'Yet he who reigns within himself, and rules passions, desires, and fears, is more a king,' but then I think the better setting would be on Venus than Earth."

Riesman's eyes widened even more. *Just when you thought things couldn't get any stranger!*

Perez smiled and returned to his calm, kindly self. He shook his head, pulled out his tablet and placed it on the table while Dee Dee spoke to the two younger women.

"Your growth here and experience will serve both of you well, Milites Vespere and Lux. I will miss you. I feel much better leaving you both here to continue the work and the replacements' training. Still, I long to see my family, to start teaching and continue my own journey. My departure will mean your promotion to Immunes."

"Thank you kindly for your patience and time, Centurion," Vespere said and bowed her head.

"You will be remembered along with my kin. Your words have been my life," Lux said.

Okay... this is crazy! Venus ... Earth? Centurion and leaving... Quoting Milton and Conrad ... all right, everyone, it's been nice getting to know you all. Time to go! Riesman pulled her napkin from her lap, plopped it on the table, and stood ready to leave, but Perez's even tone and matter of fact words caught her attention.

"All right, ladies, it looks like the authorities will be here in thirty seconds. Five agents and an unarmed man in the back, also an armed helicopter coming in from the east about one klick out.

I'm guessing it's for suppressing fire if necessary. Local law enforcement has already set up a perimeter in the front and back, leaving exits gamma and omega open. Entry will be the front door. They'll probably use flash-bangs."

Riesman's heart jumped several beats, and sweat burst through nearly every pore of her body. *How did he know they are coming? And why are they coming?* She'd thought this was only reconnaissance.

"Did the Keeper deactivate Riesman's devices?" Dee Dee asked. The three women stood in unison, pushed their chairs in, and stood behind them while Perez did the same thing.

"What? How do you know about that?"

"All but a tracking device located… really, Bobbie Jo? They made you put one there?" Perez said, pointing below her waist. Riesman's mind went blank and heat flushed her face and neck.

"Well, now, that is inappropriate," Lux said with disgust on her face.

"So much for dignity," Vespere added.

"Stop it! How … how could you know that?" She suddenly wanted to cover her front as if she were naked.

Perez made a hand signal and the women lay on the floor, closed their eyes and covered their heads while he continued. "All right, ladies, it's going to happen soon. I hope you got a plan for that rotor, Dea Data?"

"Yes, though timing and placement will be critical."

The mention of flash-bangs was enough to convince Riesman to imitate everyone else. She lay on the floor, facing away from the door with her head covered and her eyes squeezed shut.

"Good … I'm guessing flash-bang in five, four, three, two, one …"

Riesman covered her ears and waited. She was about to look up when the front door crashed open, lights flashed, something popped loudly, and heavy feet ran towards them, shaking the floor.

The events would've completely disoriented and immobilized her had she not been prepared. All she could think about amidst the noise, yells to remain still and something pressing on her body was how Perez saw this happening and with such detail.

What, or who, is the Keeper?

"Get up!" a man yelled.

The smoke and smell of discharged electricity made breathing difficult and her movement slow, but two strong hands pulled her off the ground and stood her on her feet. Riesman blinked, but it didn't clear her disorientation or stop her eyes stinging. A man bound her hands roughly in front of her. The room spun around her, making her unsure of her footing. The other women were crying.

"It's nice to see you're in one piece," Administrator Damon said, his calm demeanor at odds with the previous chaos.

At least the blast hadn't compromised her hearing.

The smoke cleared enough to reveal Damon standing in the middle of the mess surrounded by Agent Harper and men in expensive-looking suits, body armor and assault weapons.

"You could have knocked, Administrator. I'm sure Mr. Perez would have let you in." *Because somehow he'd known they were coming.*

"Perhaps ..." Administrator Damon said. "Agent Harper, please release the director and the women. I think we have the prize. Not the big one but ..."

"Absolutely."

A loud pop pierced the air and blood splattered across Riesman's face and dress. Stunned, she stared at the mess with wide eyes. One of the women screamed, and she looked up in time to see Damon fall to the ground. Shock rooted her to the spot, but the other women's cries pushed her to speak.

"What's wrong with you, Harper? You just killed my boss!" she blurted out. She glanced back and forth between the dead body, Agent Harper and Perez, and after a few moments realized she'd stopped breathing.

"Merck! Daniels! Shut those ugly pigs up," Harper said. Ignoring her, he stepped over Damon's body, his smoking semi-automatic handgun still in hand, and stood in front of Perez. Fired by adrenalin, lack of air and shock, Riesman stepped towards him, but someone yanked her back into place. Another man struck Dee Dee from behind, sending her face first to the floor. Everything moved so fast and changed so suddenly that it was impossible to take it all in. Riesman decided to focus on one thing as a time. She watched Harper, who continued to stare at Perez.

"Nice job, Jones. Teach Merck and Daniels not to hit like girls later, please."

Perez, bound like her and with a cut above his eye, remained silent and returned Harper's gaze without flinching. Riesman tried to figure out what to do next to stay alive—a difficult task with her dead boss and Dee Dee's still body just feet away.

"Captain Anthony Martinez Perez, after years of soul searching, research and interrogations, I think *you* are either the mysterious Christine Reich, or you know exactly who she is and where I can find her." A menacing smile grew on Harper's face until a flood light from a helicopter streamed through the panoramic window. Its beams gave an eerie look to the shattered apartment, and the rotors shook the plate glass.

"Harper? It's Lee. Get the package to the chamber. The locals are getting curious. No need for the others," a disembodied voice said from a small transceiver on Harper's tactical vest. Without taking his eyes off Perez, he gave the helicopter the thumbs-up.

No need for the others... Riesman thought, realizing that she had just attended her last supper. *They're going to kill us.* The helicopter moved off, and Perez said something to Harper that took her off guard.

"Just like you killed Dr. Nakamura, Agent Harper? It wasn't an accident."

Riesman's heart jumped. Her eyes locked on Harper. Her breathing slowed. Her head spun and her knees weakened. She felt as if she were going to throw up. Memories of laughing with Hiaki over breakfast in bed no more than two weeks before he died flooded her inner eye until she forced them down. Her boss's dead body confirmed that Harper could do it, but he gave no indication that Perez's accusation was correct.

"You killed Hiaki?" Her voice lacked strength, but her bound hands balled into fists.

Harper faced her, paused for a moment, then stepped towards her as if he were going to say something, but instead, he turned suddenly on Perez and struck him with his handgun. Blood gushed from a large gash above his injured eye, and he crumpled to the ground.

Riesman gasped. "Anthony!"

The sound of Vespere and Lux's crying heightened.

Perez blinked several times. "Yeah, you're a real scumbag." he said defiantly.

Harper extended both hands as if he had won a prize fight. "See, everyone. I told you this old guy would be strong, unlike that pathetic piece of shit, Nakamura. Man, the crying, weeping and begging that weak old man did was an embarrassment."

Riesman's shock turned to rage. Determined to kill Harper, she struggled against her bonds and tried to strike him when he drew near, but her guard restrained her.

"Yeah, this old guy won't have a heart attack like Mr. Hiaki Nakamura." Harper, his tone mocking, exaggerated each syllable of her dead lover's name.

"I'll kill you."

"Maybe, someday, but not today. Merck, let Daniels watch those crying bitches, and get the drugs and guns. Time to make this look like a party gone bad." Harper walked to Perez. "And get the tracker out of Riesman. We don't need her anymore, either," he said casually, as if he were ordering takeout, then he pulled Perez off the floor with the assistance of the guard who stood above him.

Someone yanked her from behind, and strong hands gripped the back of her neck and arm. "Don't worry, Director, I'll be quick."

She pulled away and spun to face him, preparing for a fight, but the guard no longer stood on the floor. Her eyes widened and her jaw dropped. One of the knives she'd admired earlier protruded through his body armor and lifted him off his feet. Riesman backed away from the fearsome weapon.

A blur raced across the room and smashed into Merck's his back. His thighbones crashed into the dining room set.

Riesman flinched from his high-pitched screams. "Christ! What?"

Thrown from behind, the man with the knife in his chest crashed into another guard. Dee Dee cut Merck's screams short by cracking his exposed head open on a dinner bowl. Perez wrestled over a gun with his guard, and Riesman stepped forward to help him, but Harper blocked her way. She jerked her bound hands upwards and struck his gun hand. The weapon discharged. She grabbed his gun with both hands, expecting a struggle, but his arm lost strength, and he fell on top of her.

"Get off me, you bastard!" She shrugged him off, ready to strike again, then gasped at the sight of the two swords that cut deep into his torso, eviscerating him. Horrified by the gore, she turned in time to see Lux flick her wrist at the man struggling with Perez. A large knife magically appeared in the man's chest. His death throes tightened his finger on his weapon's trigger and set off a volley of bullets.

"Shit! Full auto!" she yelled, rolling out of the stream of bullets. But his line of fire followed her. She smacked into a pillar, thinking that she'd lost any chance of escaping death, but the man's gun arm suddenly separated from his body. Behind him, Vespere dropped a machete and helped Perez up. Behind Vespere, another man rose off his feet, swung upside down, and crashed to the floor.

Adrenalin flooded her body, and Riesman's mind spun. How had three tiny women killed five highly trained assassins in under a minute?

Beams of light flooded the plate glass windows, and they exploded with a burst of gunfire from the helicopter. Riesman hugged the floor behind her pillar as bullets flew everywhere. She caught sight of Dee Dee flashing rapid hand signals. Riesman followed her gaze. On the other side of the room, Vespere and Lux held their former attackers' assault weapons and opened fire. The helicopter backed up but continued to shoot. Luckily, the apartment's columns were more than decorative, but the hail of bullets still ate into them, trying to get at Vespere and Lux.

Riesman raced to Perez, her eyes widening when she saw Dee Dee run full speed at the helicopter, poised to hurl the spear she'd admired earlier. The helicopter moved closer, blasting the column Vespere and Lux used as cover. Dee Dee slid to a stop and hurled the javelin. The missile sailed through the apartment's broken glass and smacked into the helicopter's cockpit, shattering the protective canopy. Riesman figured it hit either the pilot or co-pilot/gunner, because the helicopter stopped shooting and veered downward.

A moment later, it crashed into the ground a few floors below and exploded, sending up an impressive plume of flames and smoke. Bodies littered the silent and shattered apartment. Had she not fought in skirmishes in Iran and had Naval and FEMA disaster training, she would probably have retched. Riesman counted the bodies and stopped at Harper. Even amid the horror, she still hated him.

"I guess it was your time to die, you asshole." A firm hand on her shoulder pulled her back to reality.

"We must go," Dee Dee said. Vespere helped Perez to his feet, and Lux headed towards the bedroom area. Dee Dee cut Riesman's binds.

"Are you Epsilon Force? The all-female Delta Force I said was bullshit?" Riesman felt strange, analytical and removed from the surreal scene of death and destruction.

"Yes, but not here. Time to leave."

Hands free and recovering faster than she expected, she followed Vespere and Perez to a bedroom on the other side of the apartment. All three women had removed their outer garments and now wore form-fitting black attire with various leather straps and belts in key areas that exposed their svelte but muscular forms. Dee Dee walked before her and Lux came back to cover the rear.

"You changed," Riesman said.

"You noticed. Time for you to lose those shoes. I have no idea how you women wear them." Lux grabbed Riesman's feet and, having no energy to fight for her one hundred and eighty-two dollar high heels, she let the woman rip them off. What would the next steps be? she wondered. Go to the police? The FBI? Who?

"A spear was your weapon of choice?" Perez said weakly to Dee Dee.

"A highly crafted, augmented javelin with reinforced shaft and copper tip, yes, the spear was my first and best option. I regret I will never get it back and that the Earthers will not appreciate its craftsmanship." Dee Dee opened up a large trapdoor that led to the floor below.

Now that's really weird ... just like everything else.

Dee Dee helped Perez down first, then Vespere spun her around and, using a large knife in one sweeping blow, cut a high slit in her beautiful dress.

"Hey! You could have killed me," Riesman said, looking at the height of the slit. As expected, it allowed her to move freely, but Riesman discovered that wasn't the primary reason for the ruined dress.

"Are you going to make me take that tracking device out of you, or are you going to do it?"

"Oh." Riesman squatted down and searched for the end of the device but felt very awkward and exposed. After turning slightly for more privacy, she produced the little transceiver/transponder and held it in her hand for Vespere to see.

"I don't want it for a keepsake, Riesman. Throw the thing over there."

Heat flushed Riesman's face—of course she didn't want it! She tossed the device against the wall, then wiped her hands on her ruined dress and was about to ask where they were going when Vespere's small, strong hands pushed her off balance. She fell, but instead of hitting the floor, she plummeted through the trapdoor, barely clearing its edges, and landed firmly in Lux's cable-like arms.

"You can afford to miss a meal, Riesman. All that sugar, rice and processed food will do you in," she said as she pushed Riesman off.

Vespere jumped through the trap door and landed solidly on her legs. The heavy door closed above them.

"Thanks for the warning." No one replied, and Riesman wondered if they understood sarcasm. She followed the others across an empty room and through a door into the public hallway. As soon as they stepped into the common area, Dee Dee, who was helping Perez, pulled a fire alarm. Sirens screamed and red lights flashed.

The hallway began to fill with nervous people evacuating, and the group walked away from the elevators and into another apartment. Once inside, Dee Dee turned to Vespere. "Blow the apartment."

She produced a small device that emitted green light, flicked a switch, and pressed a button. The light changed to red and a huge explosion rocked the building above them and to the far right. They moved on before the shaking and sound subsided.

"Okay. So you're an Epsilon Force from where? UK?" Riesman asked under her breath.

"We are not from around there either," Vespere said.

"Let me guess ... the apartment was set to blow. So you were prepared," Riesman continued, aware that her familiarity with Seals helped her adapt quickly from Thanksgiving dinner conversation to an elite commando unit on a mission.

"Yes," Lux replied.

Perez and these women left nothing out, nothing to chance and made no mistakes. And they killed an entire FBI strike team. But they couldn't be FBI. They'd planned to kill her, and the three women, just like they had Damon and Hiaki. Riesman wondered what she'd fallen into.

Lux opened a closet door and pushed the back wall. It opened into another part of the building, where they walked through more empty apartments. Once in a different public hallway , Vespere pulled another alarm. People came out in waves, and Riesman and the team flowed onto the street with everyone else.

Outside, large numbers of people milled around, and in the confusion, they didn't notice three small women wearing all black helping an injured man and a barefoot woman covered with blood. Riesman glanced behind her. A large police barrier obstructed the road nearly half a block away. Above her, helicopter wreckage was embedded in the third floor, and two stories above that, the penthouse burned. Brilliant yellow and white flames curled skyward and spread across the entire top floor. *Impressive.*

She turned her gaze to the front and walked on with Lux at her side. "Where are we going?"

"To a very fast vehicle," Lux replied.

"And that fire back there?"

"A little something-something I concocted to not only burn rapidly but to such high temperatures that it should melt metal, bone, teeth and everything around it. They won't be able to identify anyone. If they know we were all there, they should believe that we are all dead. Hopefully, they won't make the connection unless they find the trap door, which was at the epicenter of the blast." Still smiling at her handiwork, she opened a car door and assisted Riesman into the back seat with Dee Dee and Perez. Lux and Vespere climbed into the front. Dee Dee, observing Perez closely, removed blood-soaked bandages and replaced them with clean ones. Only then did Riesman realize that Perez had been hit.

"Oh my God!"

"Not to worry, Riesman. Two bullets cleared vital organs though one looks like it collapsed a lung. If we get him to the ship quickly, he should be fine once we clear the landing zone. Vespere, go to the emergency extraction zone on the island; we are going to the old fort in Boston Bay. *Silent Star Falling* has made all of its pickups and is already preparing to land, but it has only five windows to accomplish this between the Earthers planes traveling over it and the possibility of pursuit. There is a small landing craft exposed to open ocean that will take you to the yacht."

"Excellent! We'll be able to go fishing. I love the ocean," Lux said as the car took off at a fast clip.

"The chart, course, and supplies are all in place. Once I leave, take the new Milites and Dr. Riesman to the new location and continue with the preparation. Also, the Keeper apparently left three pounds of chestnuts for you both in the boat."

"Praise the Keeper and may she have long life!" Lux cried.

Riesman swam in a sea of information with no idea of what to do. Should she make a break for it once the car stopped, or continue on with them? After all, throughout everything, Perez and these women could have let her die—a couple of times. But they hadn't.

She looked at Perez. He appeared to be unconscious. It hit her how brutally Agent Harper had killed her boss right in front of her and brazenly admitted to killing Hiaki. She realized that the people she could trust might be only the ones with her right now. "Damn it," she said quietly.

~

November 23, 2023, A.D.... 71 minutes later

"I'm so sorry for all of this, Bobbie Jo." Perez spoke with difficulty from where he lay on the back seat of the car. Riesman knelt beside him with the door open, her back towards a large open field. His face had swollen, and bandages and compresses covered his body.

"Don't talk, Anthony. You're working on one lung ..."

Perez's frowned as if trying to remember something. "It makes sense that you take over ... Roberta Joanne Riesman: retired Major, Executive Director of Readiness, Disaster Logistics, Office of Response and Recovery at FEMA, US Office of Naval Intelligence, Ph.D. Psychology, MPH ... it makes sense ... you'll understand the issues ... the disaster, hysteria ..." he muttered.

Not knowing what to do, she put her hand on his shoulder. It seemed to bring him back to the present, and they sat quietly for a moment in an empty field in the middle of an abandoned fort in Boston Bay.

"Just rest, Anthony. I guess help is coming," Riesman said.

He nodded and closed his eyes.

She surveyed the open, desolate field tucked at the end of a peninsula. A Civil War fort stood in ruins on a nearby hill overlooking the vacant field and ocean. Light swept across the sky from the automatic lighthouse beside it, and faint light from the Boston skyline bled through the fog. Riesman took a deep breath, and the refreshing smell of sea salt, ocean and some kind of flowers eased her tension.

I'm alive.

Only the constant flow of air traffic heading over the island into Logan International Airport marred the setting. The roar of engines moved from a distant hum in the east to a loud thunder as they passed low overhead, and then faded as the planes coasted in for landing. Always another plane followed right on their tail.

Dee Dee stood by the driver's door staring at her tablet while Vespere and Lux organized back packs, five of them by Riesman's count.

This is an operation. Some kind of extraction, she thought. *How many times have I been here ... usually with my own gear and boots ...*

Cold rose through the soles of her mangled shoes, and Riesman's heart grew heavy as she tried to figure out what to do next.

As if reading her mind, Perez spoke quietly but clearly. "You know you can never go back, Bobbie Jo. Those people back there are killers. They killed Hiaki and your boss with ease. You and the other girls were on the list, and I would have joined you shortly, I'm sure."

"I can go to the police. I have friends in D.C. ..."

"And then the same people that set your boss up, interrogated Hiaki, and killed them both would find you. They would assume you know something."

Riesman raised her voice above the airplane noise. "But I don't know anything!"

"I know that, Bobbie Jo. I know that," Perez said. "But they don't. And these are the kind of people that don't like loose ends. The people who sent that hit team don't know how much or how little you know, and they won't be happy until you're dead."

Riesman tried to find fault with his logic, but considering that she'd escaped death less than two hours ago after being compelled to be a part of entrapping a German national, Perez's analysis seemed accurate.

"But what about my family? My sisters and nieces ..." Yet another plane rumbled in the distance.

"They'll be safe if you're presumed dead. If they think you're alive, they become bait."

Perez shuffled across the seat towards the door. Taking the cue, she assisted him outside, and he leaned on the car facing the field, looking settled but tired. The sound of the plane overhead receded and, surprisingly, none took its place. Riesman looked east and didn't even see any navigation lights.

"Looks like my ride is here. Do me a favor and hold onto this until I get back." Perez handed her his tablet. "I may get a new one, but I want you to hold onto this because it belongs here, and it will help you with some answers. I'm going to be gone for a while."

She frowned. "Anthony? What are you saying?"

"Right now it's rebooting and should be back online in about a week. The transmissions are weak and it desperately needs recharging," he explained.

Though reluctant to touch it in light of what happened last time, she took the tablet. The night had grown strangely still, the roar of descending planes having ceased. She turned and looked east again—no oncoming planes, just an empty field.

She turned back to Perez with a frown. He took a deep breath, as if the prior conversation had exhausted him, and pointed directly upward. She looked up and gasped, eyes wide, heart suddenly racing. Above them, a massive, black bird silently descended. Riesman took a step back, shaking her head in disbelief. A moment later, landing gear emerged from the smooth, black ship.

Earthers, Terrans, Venus, not alone in the universe ... spaceships? Another planet?

"Holy Crap! My God! What in God's name is that?" Riesman said with bated breath.

Dee Dee provided a casual explanation of the vehicle in standard military, minimalist vernacular while she assisted Perez. "An interplanetary, stealth spaceship typically used for observation, surveying, immediate evac, and pickup runs. Minimal weaponry so it's very fast while having a guidance and landing system that uses the Earth's molten core and magnetic field as a means of landing rather than the usual chemical fission thrusters required on Terra and Venus. Due to Earth's rapid rotation, the magnetic field alone will suffice for lift off."

Slack jawed and wide eyed, Riesman watched the massive ship settle on landing struts, and felt a sudden need to go the bathroom.

"Immunes Vespere and Lux—you're now in command. If all goes well, I'll see you both in ten years or less. Good luck and instruct your Milites well," Dee Dee said as she helped Perez to the opening ramp. Both women stood silently at attention and placed a closed fist over their heart in salute.

This can't be happening! A spaceship? For real?

"Bobbie Jo? Bobbie Jo—go with Vespere and Lux. They'll make sure you're safe. Once the tablet recharges, it'll tell you what you need to know. Then you can make your own decisions," Perez said.

Slowly, Riesman recovered from the shock. With Dee Dee's support, Perez ambled to the ship. Two other women that looked just like Vespere and Lux passed them at the edge of the ramp.

"Let me come with you." Riesman spoke out of desperation, not even sure what she meant. Dee Dee and Perez stopped and looked back at her, obviously as surprised as she was for asking.

"Hiaki is dead. I'll have to hide and never see my family. There's nothing to stay here for," Riesman blurted out as tears filled her eyes.

Perez motioned her closer. "Bobbie Jo, if you hear what the Keeper tells you, you may decide to take a path that will create an entirely different and more important life than you could ever imagine. I'd hoped to be around, but this is your place, here on Earth, while I need to be elsewhere with my daughter. As long as you have the Keeper and your team, you'll never be alone unless that's the journey you take."

Riesman shook her head. His words hadn't reassured her, and she had too many unanswered questions. Where was his daughter? And who is this Keeper?

"Have faith in yourself. Trust me, you're the right person for this. Even if they call you Giant, the role you'll play with this planet's history is monumental. You're actually trained for this kind of change, both the real dangers and the more ... existential one. " He and Dee Dee ascended the ramp, and it started to close. Riesman stepped out of the way, feeling suddenly alone, empty, and exhausted. The ramp closed, and the struts silently retracted.

"No ... don't leave me here alone."

"You're not alone, Riesman. You do not have to be unless that's what you wish." Vespere said in a quiet and unusually gentle voice. Riesman turned. Vespere was looking up, watching the large ship slowly ascend as quietly as it had descended.

A few moments later, the black spaceship was nearly invisible, and planes flew in again from east to west. Riesman's gaze fell to the ground. She felt as if she were going to weep.

What am I going to do?

A familiar voice jolted her. "Vespere! The new Milites—Bella and Pax? They have never been on the sea, which does make sense, considering! They are in for such a treat," Lux said from behind her. She looked back to see the two new women donning the packs she'd seen earlier.

"Is it true about how there are chestnuts and lemons that fall from trees and are just left there?" the new soldier, Bella, asked eagerly.

"All true. And there is more, including great fishes in the ocean which you will see. Now we must go—the chestnut and lemons await us on the yacht, but we must clear the bay and be in open ocean before daylight," Lux said.

Riesman glanced at her tablet. It looked like a solid piece of black stone.

"I can imagine that this is all confusing, Riesman.'

She looked up. Vespere held another pack, opened for her to see shoes and clothes inside.

"At the very least, take these clothes and come with us for a short while, until the Keeper talks to you. Then make your decisions," she said in a calm, kind voice.

Riesman glanced from her to the clothes, then took the backpack. What other option did she have? Vespere turned her back to give Riesman privacy.

"Thank you." Riesman put the heavy backpack down and took out a warm jumper and track pants—much more appropriate than her torn dress for going on a yacht.

"Yes, but in all fairness, I suspect that like many of you Earthers you are nearly hairless all over ... which is simply too much for me," Vespere said. The disgust in her voice was so obvious that Riesman stopped in mid-stride to rewind the last comment to make sure she understood what Vespere said.

"Well, of course, I have some hair on my legs when I don't shave, but the only hair I have is—"

"Please, no more! The image of a hairless woman is difficult to get rid of once envisioned. I would like to enjoy my breakfast tomorrow."

An airplane roared overhead. Riesman shook her head in amazement and went back to changing clothes.

Three hours ago, she'd wanted to leave an awful Thanksgiving dinner to get away from these people. Now she was going on a cruise with female ninjas from a silent spaceship.

And it's my being hairless that's a crazy thought? What have I gotten myself into?

Chapter Six

ANDREA PEREZ, HANDS DEEP in her pockets, walked to the Great Library with a heavy heart. She figured it had to be after Thanksgiving on earth. The Christmas stuff would be out in the malls—baby Jesus in his manger, the three Wise Men surrounding the Son of God, and carols floating in the air.

Unable to sleep, she'd taken to getting up early and doing her new calisthenics routine. Normally, she would wait until the fourth shift broke from work, but today was different. She'd discovered that there was more to the solar system than Terra. More than the hand of God. Mortal beings, not God, designed life as she knew it.

"Is there a God?" The dark carpeted walkway, empty and quiet, hushed her voice. The fourth shift had hours before their morning meal when the first shift took their place, and the sentries had passed her twenty minutes ago near the residence habitat. She walked with measured steps, thinking of the past, present and future—dark thoughts that matched the concourse's low lighting.

Jesus Christ's birthday. Son of God. It was easy back then with only one planet and no intelligent life anywhere but Earth. And humans were the ones made in God's image.

But now ... What else am I going to find? Were we a mistake, too?

Her anxiety increased with every step towards the library and its books that challenged her notions of herself and her place in the universe.

Bad enough that there is Terra, but life on Venus too?

Perez stopped. She'd been so busy with her existential thinking that she'd lost track of where she was, and it felt strange to see the food courts and markets closed, but a quick scan of the area confirmed that she was on track to her destination. She noticed new edged weapons—short swords, javelins and serrated knives—with their impressive blades placed in breakaway clips hanging on racks throughout the hall, an indicator of either a great hunt preparation or a recent attack by the huge rats. Rattus! She hated those things.

She glanced down and felt along her waist. "Damn it! I forgot my sidearm again. When are you going to learn, dumbass?" But her fingers found her sheathed combat knife, a gift from Dux Cloelius for her journey and protection. She walked on and picked up her pace at a rustle behind her. She remembered her conversation with Clematis and the recent increase in rattus attacks. Perhaps such a late sojourn to her studies wasn't a good idea.

Perez stopped a hundred feet from the library. An air vent just to the left of the door hung off its hinges, as if pushed from the inside.

"Damn it."

Perez backed away to the weapons rack she'd seen several feet back. She kept her eyes peeled for any movement and cocked her head, listening, but the continuous vibration of the air and heating machines made it difficult to hear anything subtle. When she reached the weapons rack, the tension in her chest eased a little. She grabbed two large, serrated blades just as a loud, guttural scream pierced the stillness.

"Percutiamque vos monstra!"

"Damn it!"

Perez's grip tightened around her weapons, and she moved in the direction of the yell, eyes darting everywhere. Glass shattered below her level, followed by the sound of breaking wood, perhaps a chair or table. Without thinking, she ran down the flight of stairs, taking several steps at a time. She burst onto the lower stores level and caught her breath at the sight of a young Terran girl, maybe a teenager, waving her weapon at four rats the size of large dogs with ugly tails that doubled their size. She'd seen skulls, skins and tails of these creatures hanging up to dry, but their similarity to the smaller versions on her former planet surprised her. Only their huge size made them grotesque and evil monsters, and seeing four of them surrounding a young woman pushed Perez from shock to disgust to loathing and hatred. Anger burst from her heart and she let go a scream of her own.

"No!" She ran, clutching the hilts of her blades, into the battle. Her first blade crashed into the back of one rat as it turned to face her, and her second blade struck out at the rat's nose. For a moment, Perez felt disoriented, as if she'd bumped her head, then something stung her right side. She ignored the sensations, yelled again, and struck out at the retreating creature. To her satisfaction, it scurried away with one of her blades sticking out of its back.

Screw you, bitch!

With one out, she shifted her focus to the others. Two of the rats slunk off, startled by her appearance, but the third seized the moment of distraction and snapped at the young woman's hand. Her blade clattered to the ground, along with several of the fingers that had gripped it. The woman grimaced but didn't scream. She just tried to grab her fallen weapon with her other hand, while the rat devoured her fallen fingers. Perez, shocked by the girl's stoicism, yelled and tossed her remaining edged weapon to the girl, then drew her combat knife. Perez glanced at her small weapon and realized she needed more. Without a thought, she grabbed a broken chair leg and attacked the rat as it made a run at the girl. Though losing blood, the girl, clearly well trained with edged weapons, slashed out at the rodent who'd taken her fingers. After tasting blood and flesh, the rat looked determined to kill her.

"Hodie non turpis linguis! Not ever, you scum!" Perez yelled as she advanced to the woman's side, but before she got there, another rat appeared and scurried towards her. Perez screamed and swung the chair leg into the creature's legs. She heard a bone break. The rat snapped and she backed away, but she struck the creature repeatedly in the head until it stopped snapping. The injured rat stepped back, favoring its broken leg. Perez lunged and shoved her knife in the monster's eye. It screeched and flailed around, tail swinging. Perez jumped aside but the rat's tail brushed her left side and ripped her pants, cloak and skin. Nonetheless, the creature slunk off with her knife embedded in its eye. She stared defiantly at another rat that watched from the distance, and it fled along with the other two. Down to her chair leg, Perez turned to the injured girl. She looked very pale and her movements had slowed.

Blood loss, shock—shit!

The rodent hunched down, hips up, eyes focused on its victim, preparing to attack. With a scream, Perez raced in, drawing the full attention of the rodent. It bared its ugly teeth, stiffened its tail, and wriggled its haunches, about to spring. Only the young woman stopped it. She jumped on top of the creature and drove her blade deep into its back. The rat jumped, knocking the girl off, and swung around, trying to bite the blade protruding from its back. Perez swung her chair leg like a bat and made full contact with the creature's head, but her club, though solid, broke in two. Only a makeshift wooden stake remained. She grasped it firmly, but her leg began to go numb and her head ached. The young woman lay face down on the ground, not moving.

Not good.

The dazed and bleeding rat backed away from Perez and turned to the downed girl. Without hesitation, Perez stepped between the predator and its prey. She waved her stake and crouched low, bracing herself for another attack. She looked for the best place to strike. Though slowing, the rat appeared determined to have its meal.

"The underbelly ... I'll get her fingers from your stomach, you bitch!"

The creature crouched lower, once again poised to attack. Just as Perez thought she would get her shot, something struck the rat from behind. It vectored to the side and slammed into a group of tables and chairs where it remained, unmoving. Two spears and a throwing knife stuck out of its body. Perez breathed a sigh of relief and looked around for her rescuers.

"Ad arma!" A group of women yelled from the floor above. *The sentry group ... thank God.*

Satisfied that the danger had passed and help was en-route, Perez fought the banging in her head and growing pain in her side and strode towards the young woman with one leg trailing. The numbness was spreading.

"It would've been so much easier if you had your sidearm," she said to herself. She made it to the young woman and turned her over to make sure she was still alive. Not sure, Perez ripped off her blouse's sleeves and made a tourniquet for the woman's wrist. Every time she looked down to attend to the woman, something dripped from above, and she wondered where it came from. The first responder arrived with her weapon still drawn. She stopped and stared wide-eyed. Perez finished her work on the injured girl, then looked right back at the staring woman.

"What ..." Perez started to say, but the effort winded her.

Three more women arrived. They too stared at the scene, jaws slackened as if in awe. The first woman's expression changed from surprise to a broad smile at their reaction. Perez ignored them and took a deep breath for the first time since the battle. She felt drained; her leg felt dead, her side was on fire, and her head hurt. She put her hand on her head to see what was dripping on her and assumed the warm liquid was sweat.

She tried to speak, but her voice sounded different. "That young woman is hurt and she needs medical attention. Now." Perez lowered her hand and stared, eyes widening at the blood and hair smeared across it. She did remember feeling disorientated at one point, as if something had hit her. Perez looked back at the woman. She'd sheathed her weapon and the other three had gone to take care of the young woman and look for the other rats.

"There will be such a lore about this, Earther. You have no idea what you have done. You are now Terran—battle-hardened and bound by blood to a noble name," she said solemnly.

Beyond her hand, a pool of Perez's blood puddled around her injured leg. "Oh hell," she said, recounting how many times she might have been struck.

The woman continued speaking, but Perez, swimming in confusion, didn't register the words. Her eyesight tunneled, and she felt as if the ground rushed up to meet her. Strong arms stopped her from crashing into the ground. Tiredness overwhelmed her and she drifted off.

Chapter Seven

Earth. December 5, 2023, A.D.

RIESMAN TURNED OVER IN her snug bunk. Resting had given her a chance to put the Thanksgiving events behind her or, at least, to take a break from thinking about them. She'd already slept a couple of hours, but her new alien women friends were singing and dancing above deck louder than usual. Under normal circumstances being on a yacht anchored at Bimini just west of the Bahamas would be enjoyable, especially in December, but restlessness, anxiety about the future, and knowing things she preferred not to know about spoiled it for her.

"Really? A hidden world with more of those people?" she said aloud, her voice competing with the festivities above. Satellite news and internet reports that she and Administrator Damon, along with a number of guests, were presumed dead from a horrific fire made everything seem more real. She snickered at the constant reports from a Christine Reich's spokesperson in Hamburg who reported that 'Ms. Reich never made her flight out to be at that party,' and that she was 'saddened by the terrible events.'

Lucky you. Several dead, assassins killed, intended victims MIA, and world's biggest secret revealed. It's the best flight you ever missed.

But the four women on the boat distracted her from the truth of that night. The new arrivals acted like children in a toy shop, delighted by their fresh experiences—the ocean, chestnuts, lemons and fish. Meal times had a festive atmosphere, filled with laughter, singing and talking about their own planet, Terra.

Riesman learned that the tidal-locked planet on the other side of the Sun had advanced technology to hide it from Earth, but the technology was failing. If she hadn't seen the spaceship silently landing and lifting off, and the similar, though alien, nature of the women around her, she would've thought such ideas meant she was high or psychotic.

Yet, it was all real. She knew, but the rest of the world didn't, and it would be chaos when it found out. How could Jesus Christ save another species when he was the human son of God? People would ask. *Genesis? We're supposed to be special, a chosen people in the image of God.*

In addition to the existential dilemma, the aliens liked to walk around naked. They couldn't do it on their home planet, but Earth was apparently ideal for the lack of clothes. And to Riesman's surprise and chagrin, they took great pride in their bodies. It took her several days to learn not to stare. Nearly every part of their bodies had hair except for their breasts, the majority of their face and neck, and the back parts of their limbs. The hair on their head was thick and coarse, while their body hair appeared fine and silky. She discovered that her walking around in a one piece bathing suit was just as revolting to them. To reduce the mutually discomforting visual images, Riesman spent much of the day topside, enjoying the sun and clearing her head with either Lux or Vespere, while the others slept, rested and worked below. Unfortunately, that meant they typically stayed up at night, all night, navigating the vessel and partying as if on spring break.

The days slipped by, and they stayed very close to Bimini. It finally dawned on Riesman to ask why they were there.

"This may be overwhelming," Vespere said.

"Really? It may be 'overwhelming?' After seeing an

interplanetary spacecraft and everyone talking about their home planet being on the other side of the Sun, I don't think there's much more that can surprise me," Riesman said honestly.

Vespere's sigh indicated that she was choosing her words carefully. "This site still holds an active Keeper's communication node. The Keeper of Earth was located in a land your people called Atlantis. When it was swallowed by the ocean, all of its secrets, teachings, and population were killed, leaving only a partially functioning node, a remote computer. The tablet you hold is a portal or mini-computer that accesses this node. Since it was in constant use for the last decade, it shut down. Once this happens, the portal, or what you have been calling the tablet, needs to be brought here so it can recharge, update and reboot. That's why we rushed to get here. This is why we stay, other than the beautiful location and weather." Vespere stopped and sat quietly.

Unable to find words, Riesman sat with the sun warming her shoulders and neck and stared at the naked, hairy Vespere and her beautiful ocean backdrop. Eventually, she nodded and went below deck to sleep. Perhaps she was suffering from heat stroke.

"Atlantis … the City of Atlantis? See what happens when you think you've heard everything," she said. Riesman hoped that sleep would help her perspective.

She slept well beyond dinner, and, once awake, decided to stay in her bunk in an attempt to fit another puzzle piece with everything she'd learned to date. Her fear of how the general population might deal with the revelations of a new planet, a new species and its relationship to Atlantis, tired Riesman in spite of the dancing and singing above decks, and her eyelids started to close. They flew open when electric blue light suddenly illuminated the small room.

"Roberta Joanne Riesman. Thank you for transporting me to this location for rebooting and recharging," a calm female voice said. Riesman bolted upright, narrowly missing the cabin's ceiling.

The tablet Perez had given her glowed. "Updates are complete, and we can now leave this location. Would you like a mission briefing?" the voice continued.

Bleary-eyed and still sitting on her bunk, Reisman took a moment. "What?"

The tablet's light subsided to a low intensity dark blue. Riesman turned on the light. The tablet looked different; blue rather than the glossy black she remembered. *It speaks ... and it changed color.*

"Immunes Riesman. You are obviously still confused, either from your sleeping or the entirety of these past events that have resulted in you needing to give up one life for that of another. I will take the initiative and provide a very brief synopsis of the mission," the voice said.

"All right," Riesman said cautiously.

She slipped from her bunk and stood over the tablet, watching the images that accompanied the voice—DNA coding, physical structures of humans along the evolutionary line, and then two worlds, Earth and another that looked less hospitable.

"You may call me Keeper, as I am the portal to the last remaining power node of the Earth's only Keeper in Atlantis. I should remain functioning for the next decade depending on use. Here is a summary:

"There are two habitable planets in this solar system remaining from a total of four. Terra was an experimental habitat that was never expected to survive but has persevered as a result of the Terran Keeper, the Architects and Eco-Scientists. It is inhabited by a species similar to humans you know as Terrans. These Terrans are a separate hominid species from planet Earth. They may appear as derivatives of what you would label as Neanderthal, but this species predates human development on this planet. The original Terran species developed on Venus until the cataclysmic events created by its greenhouse effect necessitated their relocation to Terra permanently. As Terra's original species died out, the eco-scientists groomed the present Terran species to inherit the planet.

"The events that destroyed Mars, home of our creators, the 'Originators,' also wiped out the dinosaur species of your planet and accidentally furthered Earth's development. The planet's atmosphere stabilized approximately sixty-three million years ago, and the Eco-Scientists moved five hominid species to Earth in the hopes that one of the species would survive and thrive. Ultimately, the planet yielded one species. However, for a period of time, two coexisted and interbred. The groups you refer to as Neanderthal from Europe and southwestern-central Asia, and Homo-sapiens that evolved from Africa, produced offspring that left mitochondrial remnants that exist at an estimated point zero-zero-zero-one-three. Your mitochondrial remnants exceed that baseline, making you the closest ambassador between the humans on Earth and Terra ...."

Though she found the information fascinating, Riesman shook her head with frustration. "What does it matter? Why is it important? Why did Hiaki Nakamura have to die? What does this have to do with the women topside and Perez?" she blurted out.

The outlandish history of Mars, Venus, dinosaurs and Neanderthals filled her mind with more outrageous thoughts than she'd ever dreamed could exist. Without hesitation, the Keeper answered the questions in a calm, low tone.

"Your sharing the mitochondrial remnants is important because you have a connection to both planets that is valued by the more technologically advanced civilization of Terra. Further, in eight point five years, part of Terra will move out from the solar glare of the sun, making it visible for the first time in Earth and Terra's history. While it has been able to use the sun and a sophisticated holographic imaging device to hide the planet, the machinery required to keep the planet invisible is failing. It has required periodic shutdowns to repair but its ability to remain perpetually active is no longer possible. It will take Earth two point three months to discover Terra if its cloaking system were to fail. Dr. Nakamura's work in light, prisms and energy was on track to discover this technology. Terra wanted to bring him to their home planet with other humans to assist in repairs. He was contacted but refused to leave."

"Why?" Riesman said more than asked. "He wouldn't have been afraid. My God! He would have leapt at the chance of a new world ..." She saw his caring face with dark, penetrating and smiling eyes. How he made her so happy.

"He reported that he did not want to leave you," the Keeper said.

Riesman's heart sank and her eyes filled with tears. She couldn't move or speak. Hot tears hit her cheeks, lips and bare feet. Her mouth quivered and her knees weakened. She had no idea how long she remained that way, and only when her sniffling stopped and her crying slowed, did the Keeper's voice return.

"Once Dr. Nakamura understood the nature of his work and how Terra's discovery would affect an unprepared Earth, he agreed to destroy his work. Mr. Perez was sent to assist him in that endeavor. Once Immunes Perez discovered his relationship with you, both he and Dr. Nakamura accurately feared for your life."

Another wave of sadness washed over her at hearing both names.

They both cared for me?

"Further review of your medical file, history, and family of origin search found a remote possibility that you possessed mixed heritage. I confirmed this when you made contact with me on November twenty-third, two thousand and twenty-three. Once Dr. Nakamura's death was confirmed, your safety was compromised. Immunes Perez made contact with you in the hope that the people watching you would use you to get to him. Their ultimate goal is to find Ms. Christine Reich. The events that occurred on Thanksgiving were initiated and perpetrated by rogue agents of the United States federal government. However, Immunes Perez and his Terran team orchestrated their role. Its purpose: disrupt their efforts, create the illusion of your death, and to clear a path for you to take over as team leader vacated by Immunes Perez."

Riesman stood silently over the dimly-glowing tablet, considering the implications of the last sentences. The tear tracks on her face dried as she took in the information and processed it as if it were a complex puzzle.

"How do you know these things? How can you be sure of all these things when you're from an alien world?"

"Due to an unexpected event, we discovered Johann Christian Reich twenty-three years ago—"

"You mean *the* J. C. Reich of Reich Enterprises?"

"Yes."

"What do you mean 'you discovered him?'"

"The Terran survey ship, *Clear Ahead Horizon*, suffered systemic computer failure resulting in loss of orbit. The crew abandoned ship but not before setting the ship to self-destruct upon crash landing to ensure secrecy. This occurred in Tunguska, Siberia, Russia on Earth time-line July 30, 1908."

Something about that location was familiar.

"The eight survivors were able to remain unnoticed and covert. However, with the advent of World War Two, it was evident to the survivors that Earth technology was advancing faster than expected. The team reorganized itself and drew up new mission parameters: locate the Atlantis power node to bring me back online; re-establish communication with Terra; locate Earthers who would be in a position to understand the situation, and use our advanced technology to create an identity that would allow us to monitor all communication, access all computers and artificial intelligent creations, and access all critical commercial, military, educational and scientific forums world-wide."

"You did it, didn't you?"

"Yes."

"So when history says that Reich created the light-bearing principle that changed the way computers think…"

"We were the ones that assisted in that project as a means of tying into all future operation systems and allow Immunes Reich to increase his wealth."

Riesman's head spun as she tried to remember what else the elusive J. C. Reich did in the world of technology and computers. "It's involved in every computer on the planet now," she said.

"Yes."

"And he created the 'Licht Lagersoftware.' the 'Lucifer' software…"

"Yes. This software is key in harnessing the computer power from a computer's hard drive memory into amplifying the working memory, RAM, of any computer. Processor speed increased exponentially. J. C. Reich's transition from using my knowledge and mathematical advances moved from predicting profitable stocks in the United States to an actual technological advancement. As a result, J. C. Reich was able to move his already amassed fortunes into controlling shares in the foreign equivalents of Microsoft, Apple, Android and MaxDrive operating systems as well as acquiring these same companies' suppliers. The net result was an increase in his vast wealth and resources, as well as placement of Lucifer software in every operational computer on the planet in two thousand and eight."

"Just before the world-wide recession …" Riesman said. "He was able to move all of his money into commodities to hold its value as stocks crashed. And when they were at their lowest, he bought them all … stocks in computer, software, military suppliers, universities …"

"Yes."

"But didn't he die?"

"His fictional death was recorded to have occurred on July twenty-third, two thousand and ten, as a result of a heart attack. This left Christine Reich as sole heir to his empire."

Fictional death?

"Let me guess, J. C. is alive and well?"

"He lives as Joseph Collins in Maui, Hawaii. He adopted Terran life style and has halted his diabetes, maintained optimal weight, and reversed his high blood pressure. While he still drinks more than the recommended amount of wine per day, he is active and reports that he is having the time of his life."

"How does Perez fit in here? I mean, this is pretty incredible ..."

"His daughter, Andrea Perez, specialized in spectrograph science and gravity."

"And you found this out."

"My artificial intelligence and access points are spread over the entire planet. This includes, but is not restricted to, the US Department of Defense, NASA, the National Security Agency, the Chinese Ministry of State Security, and hundreds more databases and servers that are thought to be impervious to security breaches." The Keeper's voice was calm, matter of fact, and emotionless as it reported on how it had breached every security and defense agency in the world.

Riesman stood still and watched the corresponding images and events that the tablet relayed, including visuals from top secret bases that were rumored to exist around the world. After a few moments of silence, save for the dancing and music topside, she began to fully appreciate that this tablet had a back door to everything. The Terran software increased processor speed and was in every operating system, that meant that any private or public agency with the need for top grade computers would have it by default.

"Damn," she said. "Who is Christine Reich?"

"Christine Reich is a virtual creation, the fictional orphaned niece of J. C. Reich. Long before his reported death, I created a virtual footprint and put all his documents and assets under her control. The top ones are Reich Enterprises' computer companies, pharmaceutical companies, import-export companies, and specific electronic firms. She is real to the world but is solely virtual."

Riesman sat on the edge of her bunk, her head swimming with espionage, false identities and alien computers and worlds. She pulled the blanket over her shoulders and said nothing. She felt lost, alone, and completely out of control.

Now what? "So what do I have to do with this?"

"Your participation is voluntary. Immunes Perez believes you to be a capable person, but he did not wish to commit you to the mission unless you wished."

Riesman's heart and mood lifted. She smiled at her painted toes and felt a glimmer of hope. "I can walk away if I chose?"

"Yes. I will need to provide a new identity and a substantial amount of financial resources for you to live well and in obscurity abroad."

"A *substantial* amount of financial resources? You mean I'd be rich?"

"Yes."

"Okay." Visions of living in France jumped into her head. She could smell the cafes, feel the expensive clothes and fast cars, and taste the wine, cheese and croissants. "I wish you'd told me that part first." Her voice sounded light and clear.

The visions and sensations were perfect until she remembered her family, Anthony Perez, and Hiaki Nakamura. Her thoughts turned dark at the memory of Agents Harper and Lee killing her boss, and intending to kill her. Now that the option of leaving was a viable recourse, Riesman asked a question she did not expect to ask:

"And what if I stay?"

The Keeper spoke as evenly as before.

"You would take on the virtual life of Christine Reich. You would complete the primary missions, which are twofold: warn your world of the impending natural disaster of the significant release of methane gas emanating from the reduction of ice and permafrost in the North and South Poles and initiate steps that need to be taken prior to this catastrophe, and facilitate Earth's discovery and processing of Terra's discovery."

Methane gas? Riesman's FEMA director persona took over. She jumped off the bunk and picked up the tablet. "What do you mean, 'methane gas?'"

"Immunes Riesman, before I proceed, I need to know if you are inclined to disembark from this proposed mission or to engage it. The choice of this journey is yours."

The Keeper's matter of fact tone bothered Riesman. "So … before I hear anything more, you want to know if I'm in or out?"

"Yes. Immunes Perez chose you because he felt you would also address a number of other objectives."

"Like what?" Images of destitute children, women, and families, all in pain and distress flowed across the Keeper's screen. Riesman's eyes knitted. "What the hell is this?"

The Keeper stopped the disturbing flow of human horror and focused on a group of apparently well-off people.

"Disrupt a child trafficking operation posing as an adoption agency in Moscow, Russia. Disrupt human trafficking, prostitution and drug operation in Beijing, China. Disrupt and terminate flow of child slavery via Sir Robert Phillip Pierce of Pierce Industries, London, UK."

"Hold that image," Riesman blurted out. A regal-looking man dressed as an elf and surrounded by very young girls dressed in sheer gowns filled the screen. He smiled, but the girls did not. Perez had looked at the same man at Hiaki's funeral with intense disgust and vehemence. The reason was now clear.

"Child slavery … *Sir* Pierce."

"Yes."

Her anger swelled and she had to consciously release her tightening grip on the tablet's edges. The music and dancing above seemed to escalate as the question settled in her brain. Her confusion and ambivalence faded and the motivation that emerged caught her by surprise.

Do I want to get back at the people who killed Hiaki? Do I want to save these kids and do a little good in the world? she thought as more dossiers of 'bad' people flowed across the screen.

"I could live in peace … in France ..."

"Yes," the Keeper answered as if it were a question.

Riesman looked into the blue glare in her small cabin and struggled with conflicting thoughts. The urge to run was palpable.

"I don't know," she whispered.

Chapter Eight

Day 89, Year 42,014. C.V. Terran time line

"HOW COULD I HAVE been so blind to it all? Why did I wait so long to ask the bigger questions?" Andrea Perez said. She stood akimbo at the apex of the largest pyramid on the planet's surface in front of several feet of transparent stone windows, looking into what appeared to be a star field and empty space.

She turned and looked at the world clock and calendar on the wall several yards behind her. It announced that it would shut down the planetary cloak field in five seconds. Maintenance and repair would have to be completed in five days. Perez took these precious moments to relax in full knowledge that she and the other scientists would probably be on their feet with the engineers for that entire period.

She turned back as the rocky Terran landscape dotted with pyramids of all sizes materialized in the window. Her reflection, appearing leaner and more muscular than before her battle with the rattus, overlaid the view of the rocky surface. She stood prepared to fight, holding the hilts of two long serrated knives. Her old combat knife, retrieved from the rats by the Terrans, sat against her thigh. To complete the ensemble, she sported a handheld laser capable of eight individual shots that could cut through diamond in seconds. She'd never been without her firearm since her release from the infirmary.

She shifted focus back outside before her gaze reached the reflection of her scarred head. To her left, windswept rocks, sand and periodic pyramids glistened in the sun of the perpetual day. She thought about the revelations she'd dug up and shook her head in disbelief that she'd not pieced it all together sooner. In an effort to think of something else, she shifted her gaze to the perpetual darkness on her right where more low-lying pyramids stood against bitter winds and crackling lightning bursts. The flashes illuminated a great frozen ocean in the distance.

She took the precious moments while she waited for Clematis to reflect on her discovery of the solar system's origin. She'd spent many hours locked away in the Great Library and other libraries, including the Keeper's Chamber. Terra's world computer still worked and provided images that fleshed out the illustrations and diagrams the Terrans had produced to preserve the story. Many times she'd cried tears of joy and sadness; she'd felt bursts of understanding and then moments of darkness and confusion. Climbing aboard an alien ship to another planet was nothing in comparison to her latest discoveries.

She'd been so busy learning the new science, technology and languages, that she'd only looked at Terran's history before, not the others. But after Terra came Venus. Her Terran friends and colleagues watched her with great enthusiasm and brought her food and water, as if she were tracking her meal on a great hunt across the Serengeti.

After her battle with the rattus, Perez felt part of an exclusive club. As a result of her journey, as the Terrans called it, they suspended her duties with the holographic emitters and planetary cloaking. Terrans of all ages told the lore of her battle with the Magna Mures, Great Rats, as if she were a great warrior. The young woman she'd saved, daughter of an Elder, who'd sneaked out to look for a male friend, also achieved warrior status for her part in the fight. Both of their roles were great enough to propel them into lore, witnessed by the sentry group and the young woman's sister. Perez had come of age, and the story would transcend the ages.

The Battle of Delta Mezzanine they called it—sounds good, but it was more a skirmish than a battle. How long ago was it? After Thanksgiving but before Christmas ... Christ's birthday ... Son of God...

After the incident and her recovery, she'd returned to her research and discovered that Terrans were expected to endure at least six journeys. She'd already completed three, leaving procreation, teaching, and death on the to-do list. She changed her view from the right to the left and back again while different thoughts jumped around in her head. Along with the wisdom gained from her research came the pain of not being special.

"Intelligent design," she said quietly.

Though she focused on a series of lightning strikes across the frozen sea, she sensed that Legate Legionis Clematis stood behind her. Her odor and her light footsteps gave her away. After her battle with the rodents, her senses had become acute, honed to even the slightest of air movements. Even the constant hum and vibrations of the underworld's machinery didn't obscure them.

"I understand the wisdom of the journey. I'm almost embarrassed at my asking you to tell me. Now, with still more to learn, I'm both at peace and excited," Perez said to Clematis, still watching the elements rage silently outside while the powerful winds, thunder and hail reverberated under her feet.

"There is no need to be embarrassed, Perez. Always the curious ones are the most impatient. Your Earth origins clearly reinforce both your curiosity and your impatience. Your discipline harnessed them both and brought you to this part of your long journey. The relentless speed and vigor you pursued it with is beyond even the youngest of our youth. Amazing, I say. And in the middle of it, you endured a battle, fought alongside a Terran, saved her life by nearly forfeiting your own, and then you went back to your research. We are proud of you, Perez. Please, though, tell me what you found. I am curious as to how far you went."

Clematis sounded like a child about to hear a great story. Perez turned to look at her. She realized that her journey was never in isolation; her colleagues and friends were there with her all along.

"While the information and data of your journey is known to me, it's your interpretation that escapes us all. Your understanding is unique from ours as we have always been on Terra. You bring the perspectives of two worlds, and that is a journey that we cannot take without your help."

"My help?"

"Yes, Perez. One of your other journeys will be to teach what you have learned from your perspective. But please, tell me your insights." Clematis walked to the middle of the small room and sat cross-legged as if awaiting an interesting story. Perez joined her on the floor as shadows of lightning danced across the reinforced walls of the transparent stone windows. Perez rearranged her various weapons and sat beside her, wondering where to begin. Unable to cross her left leg due to the deep wounds still healing from the rat tail, she kept her legs straight.

"Please, Perez, do what the Earthers do so well—summarize and give the key points. I do not wish to spoil the full breadth of the story when you start teaching it to us later. I look forward to it."

My God, I've missed so much. How we've all fought our nature back on Earth; instant answers and no time for the stories.

"It started with your love of chestnuts, pyramids, and your physical appearances," Perez began.

Clematis's eyes grew wide. "I knew that would be the starting point! Please, tell me more."

"I'd always assumed that both Terra and Earth must have shared a common history at some point. The physical phenotype of the Terrans was consistent with an ancient species of hominids we called Neanderthals. We believed the species died out thirty to forty thousand years ago. The Terran's skull, the short, strong stature, large jaws, dense bones and powerful muscles and facial structure all led me to believe this, and that my species was the superior species. But Terrans are not Neanderthals. Rather you are an alien hominid, close in DNA but distinctly separate and Venusian in origin, relocated by yet another alien species."

"Yes! But then what made you revise that thought, other than you spending time with us?" Clematis asked.

"I'm embarrassed to say that it was less my observations for the last fifteen years and more my deduction, later supported by those now obvious facts. I was really slow," Perez said.

"Slow, thorough, it does not matter. How did you get to your conclusions?"

"I discovered that while us Earthers' intelligence is in our frontal lobe, the Terran's intellectual center is concentrated in the parietal lobe, safely tucked below the head rather than right up front."

"Oh. I never would have thought that's how you discovered the truth."

"Yes. That was why the doctors were so concerned about my head injuries." Perez pointed to her scarred head. It held a metal plate where a rat's tail scale had lodged during the fight. She often touched the chain around her neck where the two inch scale hung. A memento pulled from her head, the claw hung like a trophy. It had launched a fashion trend of rat scale and claw necklaces.

"But your Neanderthal species were the original Terrans. The ones we replaced," Clematis said.

Perez shook herself to refocus.

"Yes. To some degree, my discovery was accidental. But when I also discovered that the genetic percentage of Neanderthal and Terran DNA were nearly identical, I realized that the

Neanderthals were the Terrans that had made it to Earth. For a period of time we all co-existed there. And for a short time, there was interbreeding which left genetic marker in many of us hominids as well. The medical test you have here can identify these markers. We might have this technology now but we didn't when I was on Earth. While there is no Neanderthal DNA code in people from Africa's sub-Saharan plate, it must have been something when I showed up with my dark skin, Terran body and Earth-like head."

"Oh yes! We had never seen such a unique distribution of our DNA so clearly present in a dark Earther such as you," Clematis said.

"Well, you can thank my multiracial heritage for that. Clearly, there is more European influence than my parents and I thought. So once I realized that our species co-existed, I had to re-evaluate our very existence on Earth and the probability that we came from elsewhere."

"Yes. The fourth planet from the sun. What do the Earthers call it?"

"Mars. It's funny too; all of our myths, stories and even some of our science clearly point to it being an older planet that had life. Our best science fiction literature suggests an advanced civilization living on Mars, an idea supported by ancient writings throughout our history. Still, once I found the Keepers' old logs on Mars, I felt foolish for not seeing it before."

Perez rubbed her temples. She had a lot to keep her busy: charts, books, two-dimensional images, and ancient Keepers' logs all meticulously copied by hand in Latin. And while her appreciation and understanding of Latin grew in leaps and bounds, she never found out how Latin, a language from her own planet's ancient history, ended up on Terra.

Unless Latin originated here, on Terra. Maybe Mars?

"And what do the Earthers think of Mars?"

"There's nothing there. There was a great civilization there once, a Martian Master Keeper's on the surface even, but not today. Not on the surface, but underground there remain survivors of a great species called Architects and Master Keeper. I should have seen this. When you have stories of Martian invasions, hieroglyphics and ancient drawings that point to an older civilization on a red planet, you'd think we'd pick up on the clues. But anyway, I'm impressed with how the Keepers understood the dangerous nature of the universe and thought to colonize Earth, Venus and Terra. Almost prophetic when you think about it," Perez mused.

"I have always come to believe that their motivations to avoid extinction via meteor impact made sense. With two planets' orbits on a collision course between Mars and the Jovian planet, the Keepers must have known when the collision would happen and the likelihood of the ensuing planetary destruction. The asteroid belt put them in grave risk."

"Too true. The foresight, though, and the engineering and compassion to set out and populate new worlds is truly inspirational."

"Almost inspirational enough to write about it in a book? What the Bible called 'The Great Flood,' 'End of Days' and the 'Four Horsemen of the Apocalypse?'" Clematis said. While Terrans were not known for sarcasm, they still had the capacity for it.

Perez pinched her nose, ostensibly to relieve sinus pressure. Clematis's jab at Earth's religions didn't surprise her. "Don't be mean. We got the stories right, for the most part. We just didn't have the advantage of having a Keeper to fill in the context, and we left out the other books that explained key points of the Bible. Not bad for a species that had to do it all from memory."

"Like I said, the Earthers do not do well with unanswered mysteries. I have always been impressed with how your species did get much of it down in a book, a series of books, without the assistance of a Keeper. But then that's the tragedy of it all," Clematis said with sadness.

"Yes … when the end came for Mars, it wiped out Earth's Atlantis, home of the Keepers, and after millions of years—well into the era before the Egyptians—it finally sank into the sea. It is so sad and unfair …."

"Yes. And Venus … such a lush, beautiful world the Keeper tells us, the gem of all the planets. I am amazed that much of Earth survived unscathed, with the exception of Atlantis. Almost as if it were deliberately destroyed. An experiment perchance."

"Maybe. I wonder what things would have been like if we'd had a similar Keeper."

"It is amazing that your kind managed to prosper without one. A great experiment! Meanwhile, the Sun protected Terra, a desolate planet with nothing but caverns. I have often wondered, if the Keepers had been able to finish terraforming this planet, might it have been as beautiful as Venus?"

"It would have been better, but I'm guessing that since Terra always has the same side facing the sun, it would've taken an additional tens of thousands years on top of the tens of thousands they had to finish the job. I think your subterranean world, the location along the terminus line, and an ocean filled with life, protected by miles of ice, has served you well. The Keeper's regeneration of Terra's magnetic field and reduction of methane and sulfur from the atmosphere is impressive," Perez said.

Visions of massive, interconnecting machines that tied into a majority of the planet's pyramids from the planet's poles filled her head as she imagined what it would be like to switch the planetary machinery from holographic illusions and life supports to terraforming again.

The noise, heat and energy would be tough and the power consumption huge. Would there be enough power to keep the underground world going and keep the emitters online? Perez wondered. Maybe they'd planned to finish the project later and then seed the planet. She guessed they'd run out of time and had decided to preserve an underground habitat rather than create one on the surface.

"I think hiding from Earth is a good idea. On top of the culture shock of your planet's existence, Earth would colonize Terra if it was in prime condition. It wouldn't be long before humans showed up, planted flags and took it all over. Bad enough that our presence will be discovered soon, at least Terra looks like a desolate, hostile and dead planet. Even then, you know us Earthers …"

Perez's heart filled with anxiety at the thought of various Earth governments pooling resources and setting out to conquer a new world, just as Columbus did. *That didn't turn out so well for the Native Americans now, did it?* If Earth was at a tipping point, the human race would be more desperate and see the Terrans as a primitive species and a problem to be eliminated.

"Absolutely! That's where we once again share a lot in common. No matter how inhospitable the land is, we can live there. We can live anywhere. But tell me, Perez, would our existence if known to our Earth cousins be so bad?" Clematis asked.

Perez answered as if their very lives depended on how quickly she shared her concerns. "I think it would be devastating for the nine billion people on Earth. If they were to take the same journey I did, the majority of them would understand and make changes to save their own world. But religious zealots would feel threatened if they found the Keeper's knowledge and data. Humans don't do well when fundamental aspects of their understanding changes. The basis of many religious and philosophical beliefs would become unhinged, emotions would run amok, and the knowledge that we Earthers are not alone and not unique would first shock and then anger us. Many would lose their fundamental belief in God and codes of ethics."

"Like the Judea-Christian's Ten Commandments and the Tenants of the Koran," Clematis said.

Perez pressed on, feeling an urgent need to warn her friend and her adopted world of a waking giant. "Yes. As incomplete as they both are, these codes of good behaviors might be tossed aside by those who come to believe that there is no God and that we are not unique."

Anxiety and fear took hold of Perez. Her own belief that more existed after death suddenly left her, and she felt alone in the universe.

"That is all possible, Perez, but doesn't our existence reinforce the presence of God or a Divine Creator?" Clematis asked.

Perez felt as if she'd hit a wall. The idea that good or reassurance might come from the discovery of aliens just across the solar system or that humans might embrace a newly discovered world with another similar species never occurred to her. Only Earth's consistent history of conflict when one country saw opportunity with another came to mind—wars over politics, economics, and religion.

"Did the Keeper tell you where they came from?" Clematis asked.

Lightning reflected off the walls of the silent room.

"No. The Keeper reported that its earliest memories were the discovery of Mars and its teeming ecology and bio-systems of life." A suddenly realization dawned. "Life was there before they arrived."

"So how was the circumstance for life created on Mars before the Keepers' arrival?"

Perez smiled. Some of her unasked questions possibly had answers. "It looks like I have to ask more questions," she said.

"Good, Perez. It may be time for you to join my journey as I have been searching for that answer. I would like to find it before my final journey so I can tell my kin and all the other Terrans." Clematis stood, ostensibly to leave.

Perez, surprised by the invitation to join her on an important journey, followed her lead, though with some difficulty as her leg had stiffened. "What questions have you been trying to answer?" she asked.

Clematis's eyes widened slightly.

Let me guess ... it's obvious.

"Just tell me, Clematis. I'm exhausted, hungry and thirsty." Perez took time to straighten and regain feeling in her leg. She rubbed her thin face, then ran her hands through her not-so-clean hair, avoiding the new growth near her scars. Fortunately, Clematis took pity on her and answered.

"I want to know who created the Architects and the Keepers. Where did they come from? They had to come from somewhere, right?"

Perez stopped to consider the simple question. Her hands went to her knife hilts and her eyes narrowed. In the finest tradition of Earth humans, she hadn't focused on the most important questions, the ones that could yield a more unifying answer. "Hmm."

Clematis didn't wait for an answer. Apparently, she had more immediate things on her mind. "But before that journey, I hope your father brought bushels of chestnuts. We will know soon, as *Silent Falling Star* will be here in the next several hours."

"What?" Perez's voice rose. "You let me rant and rave all this time and forgot to let me know that my father will be here soon?"

"I did not forget, Perez. I chose the right time to tell you, which was now."

"Hmm." Perez rolled her shoulders. She could feel her leg again, and it had been good to talk about all this. "Lead the way,

Clematis. I need to get clean and prepare for the drums and dance."

"Excellent, Perez! Maybe you can take the lead in the dance?"

Clematis was already opening the hatch in the floor to the staircase below.

"Maybe I will," Perez said as shook the stiffness out of her sore leg to follow.

~

Day 89, Year 42,014, C.V. Terran time line … two hours later

"Seniores Perez's condition continues to improve, Minor Perez," Centurion Dea Data said.

Perez stood close to the semi-transparent cryogenic tube where she could see him sleeping. Relieved that her father was all right, she translated her updated title to figure out why her name changed.

Oh, she thought. *My dad's here.* With her father present, he was senior to her, she was once again minor. Little things like that had distracted her more often since her head injury.

Wait until he sees me ...

Dea Data, or "Dee Dee" as she was called by Clematis, continued with her summary. "We were able to remove the projectiles with ease and repair his lung. The swelling in his face has substantially subsided while he was in cryogenic stasis. To ensure his steady recovery and acclimate his body to Terran's gravity and atmosphere, I made the decision to keep him in stasis while we adjusted his chamber during his return. "

Perez nodded but remained focused on her father. He had more gray hair, but other than the bruising near his temple, he looked very healthy and even younger. Perez felt Clematis's reassuring grip on her shoulder. Cloelius looked on.

"Thank you, Centurion. And thank you for taking care of him all these years back on Earth. He looks remarkable considering all he's done and what he's gone through."

"He is a tough brute. Disciplined, focused, tenacious—I swear he is full Terran," Dee Dee said.

Perez looked back at Dee Dee and was going to ask her a question, but Dee Dee was looking over her shoulder and smiling. Perez followed her gaze, as did the others. A large Terran male, tall and very broad, drew the women's attention. His casual gait and beautiful smile made Perez feel safe. With Terran males in few numbers, seeing one was rare. The group watched him stretch out his arms and envelop Dee Dee in an embrace.

Perez looked away to be polite, but Clematis and Cloelius did just the opposite. They looked, vicariously experiencing the embrace. Not sure what to do, Perez opted to pull Clematis and Cloelius's voyeuristic stare away and remind the couple they were still in the hangar with hundreds of staring women.

"I've seen very few males here, but he's the first I've seen that is … I don't know … muscular?"

"That is because he is one of the older ones, joined to several women for our procreation efforts. When he's not involved with his tasks, he is teaching combat maneuvers, ethics and physics. He is quite the specimen," Clematis said.

"And he's quite a looker too; he has hair everywhere and his physical prowess is legendary," Cloelius added. A hint of envy and admiration glittered in the woman's eyes.

"And he wants to talk to you later, Perez. The story of your battle with the rattus horde intrigued him, and he wants to hear more about your tactics, about how you beat back four rattus; a first, by the way," Clematis said.

"It was actually two on three; one rat stayed out of the fight and I caught one by surprise while the other was already engaged ..." The couple's conversation drew Perez's attention, and she moved to the other side of her father's stasis chamber to listen in.

"Don't ruin a good story with facts," she heard one of them say.

"...Well, I am impressed that my sisters will let me have you for three whole weeks, undisturbed, after my absence for a decade. How kind," Dee Dee said sarcastically.

The way the couple hugged and smiled at each other reminded Perez of her father and mother … *a lifetime ago*. She reached out and touched the transparency just above her father's face.

"Now, Dee Dee, be kind. I tried to get more time, but your sisters are not as flexible or as generous as you. Still, forget about them and come home. I have prepared a return meal, and the family will join us in two hours," he said.

His virile build and deep voice impressed Perez. It matched his persona.

"I must oversee the cargo manifest first and debrief on the mission." Dee Dee's expression grew sad.

Clematis took a step towards the couple. "No, Centurion Dea Data. Dux Cloelius, Minor Perez and I are here for that task," she said in a warm voice. "You are to go home with your betrothed now."

"We are?" Cloelius asked. Her expression matched Perez's surprise.

"Yes, Centurion. We have this covered. Welcome home. We will find you should we have questions." As if to finalize the act, Clematis produced a tablet and stylus and began to go through the ship's manifest.

Dee Dee's eyes widened. She smiled and bowed with her closed fist over her heart. Perez saluted in return. Dee Dee grabbed her mate's hand and they left, talking together with sparkling eyes and excited gestures while dozens of people arrived to dance upon the ship's return.

They do find reason to dance.

"That was very kind, Clematis," Perez said.

Two women dressed in medical uniforms walked up and gave quick bows.

"Yes, Clematis. You were very kind to speak for us. Very kind, indeed," Cloelius said without enthusiasm, as the medical team lifted Perez's father from the stasis chamber.

"Well, that is partially true. I do have a vested interest in seeing firsthand what *Silent Star Falling* has brought to us from Earth," Clematis said.

The medical team transferred Perez's father to a transporter and took him to the medical center.

"I'm sure there will be … My word!" Clematis's eyes widened and her mouth hung open.

"What is it?" Perez asked.

Clematis said nothing. She focused on the ship's manifest for moment, then pushed the tablet into Cloelius's hand and waited, grinning and hopping from one foot to the other while casting covetous glances at the ship.

Now what? Fresh lemons? A barrel of chestnuts? No—I bet it's a barrel of honey.

"What's going on, Cloelius? I've never seem her so excited."

Perez joined Cloelius's search of the manifest for something obvious, Perez reading slower due to the Latin. She saw Dee Dee's name and realized that her name, Dea Data, meant having been given by God. Distracted, she shook her head to focus on the ship's cargo.

"Other than chestnuts, lemons, tomatoes, and several tons of live haddock and salmon ready for transplanting ... I can't ... Oh. Now I see it. Oh, Legate Legionis Clematis! You are such a child at heart!" Cloelius said.

"What is it?" Perez asked.

Cloelius looked at Perez. Her face softened and her smile grew.

Well, at least it's good news.

"Puppies, Perez. The centurion has several species of puppies in stasis. Large breed dogs we had heard of from your planet— German Shepherds, Basset Hounds, and other hunting dog species. That is why she requested the extra stasis chambers and food for the trip back. It's been nearly two centuries since we lost our last pack. We now have our dogs back, Perez. It's such a great day for us all!" Cloelius's expression made it clear that something big had changed on Terra forever.

"Oh ... great ... I hope all of you people know what goes into taking care of these creatures. I wonder if their poop will be heavier here? Yuck!"

Cloelius ignored the comment and walked to the ship with the deliberation of one approaching a sacred alter.

Perez's father loved dogs, but her own memories were mostly that of taking the dog out to poop and picking up the mess. The day she'd left home for college was the day she escaped dog duty. But in the spirit of celebration and understanding the joy these creatures would bring to the people of Terra, she stood tall with her hands on the hilts of her blades and conjured up some enthusiasm for the dogs' arrival.

"Praise the Creators and God bless us all!" she said with emphasis. The dancers continued their jubilation, the drums beat louder, and a vision of full-sized dogs appeared in Perez's mind.

Next time those rat bastards come out again, they'll have to deal with dogs too.

Perez felt for her sidearm and found it in place. "And I won't be screwing around with knives next time."

Chapter Nine

October 31, 2014 A.D.

YOU KNOW, YOU MIGHT want to answer the phone; it might be important, Reich thought, annoyed by the costume party music competing with the ringing land line.

Who owns a land line anyway? I guess it's kind of quaint. Not practical.

She stood under the watchful eye of bodyguards, waiting for the owner of the estate to climb the elegant stairs. Bored, she looked at the floor and caught sight of her breasts. *Ah, my poor girls,* she thought; *you used to be so much bigger. That's the price you pay for clean living and exercise.*

Two heavy doors across the corridor opened. A tall, thin man dressed for Halloween as King Louis XVI stepped out, snapped his fingers at her, and motioned her and the guards into the large office. Book cases, art pieces, ornate tables and knickknacks filled the dark, possibly soundproof office. The estate's owner looked right at her, picked up his drink from the desk and moved closer to where she stood in the middle of the room. He did very little to hide his annoyance.

"Well, well, well … If it isn't the elusive Christine Reich. In the flesh, no less; often heard of but never seen. I am honored you have joined us, and in costume no less," Sir Robert Phillip Pierce said.

"The pleasure is all yours."

His smile evaporated. He took a sip and starred at her, looking natural in his regal costume. Just beyond him sat his young date dressed as Marie Antoinette. She looked uncomfortable and too young for him and his party. Reich pushed her enmity aside and focused on her compassion for the girl. Even as a cat burglar with all the accessories—skin tight fabric with leather strapping and utility belt—she felt underdressed. The ensemble enhanced her tall, muscular frame as well as her smaller breasts. Though she'd tied her red hair in a tight ponytail, her only regret with her evening's wardrobe was her functional shoes with excellent support and grip. Good for climbing, but her sexy high stiletto-heeled boots would have completed her costume—stunning, fashionable and impractical.

Such a statement, though. And if I added a whip ... that would've been as sexy as hell. Hey! Focus!

With wine glass in hand and an obnoxious smirk, Pierce closed the distance between them, flanked by his two serious-looking bodyguards.

Oh yeah ... I'm supposed to be frightened.

"David, Rachael, can you believe that Ms. Reich thought she could just show up and crash my party? London's most talked about event of the year?"

"Not very proper," the female said.

"Yes. Not very polite at all, Sir Pierce," the other chimed in.

"And while you are well dressed for the occasion, I would like to know how you managed to obtain this," Pierce held up an ornate invitation.

Hmm ... that was a good forgery.

Memories of Anthony Perez talking to him at Hiaki's funeral flooded her, especially his look of disgust as Pierce and his underage date walked away. He'd looked almost as angry as she felt right now when she glanced at the minor on the couch.

Yeah ... we're not done here, you pig.

With little regard for her own safety and little attempt to disguise her loathing, she looked right into Pierce's eyes. "I'm sure that if you'd known I was going to be in town for business, you would have invited me. An oversight, I'm sure."

The guards crowded her on each side while Pierce moved to stand in front. She smiled at how calm she felt—far from intimidated—and noted various soft targets on Pierce's body should she have to move quickly.

Yeah ... these shoes were the better choice. Reich shifted her weight to her rear leg, leaving her front leg available for a kick to his stomach should the need arise. After months of altering her exercise regime to incorporate more weights, and significant training in combat skills and edged weapons, she was ready. Field tested and ready to go, she waited for any excuse to strike.

Mission first, payback second, free the girl third, she reminded herself as she tried to disengage from his attempts to intimidate her. She reviewed how she would strike him and then thought how the elimination of processed foods really did reduce anxiety, stress, and cleared her thinking.

Anthony had been right about the change in diet and food. *I swear my skin has gotten tighter too, and my hair—no more bleaching it blonde.* If she'd known she was a natural redhead, she would have dropped the processed foods long ago.

"You cost us time and aggravation, you know," Pierce said. "At least forty-five minutes to identify you without bothering my guests, and then an additional twenty minutes backtracking how you produced a legitimate invitation, and another half hour to make sure you were alone. All of my invitations are pressed and addressed under my direct supervision."

"You don't like mysteries?"

"No, I do not!"

After an uncomfortable moment of silence, Pierce snapped his fingers at his guards and turned his attention to a phone on his desk that buzzed a low, soft chime.

So you'll answer the low buzzing phone but not the loud ringing one?

"It would be easier on you if you just tell Sir Pierce where you stole it from," the female guard said into her ear.

"Yeah, much easier," the male guard added with an additional nudge at her arm. Unfazed by the guards, Reich continued her silence and stood impassively, projecting fearlessness.

"You obviously have a well-connected network and resources to obtain this, but why would you go to such lengths to simply attend a party?" Pierce continued.

His unanswered phone was really beginning to wear on her. Didn't he have people who could answer that? "Well, you did say that 'everyone who is someone will be there,' Sir Pierce."

Pierce's eyes narrowed and he stopped sipping his wine in mid-step. "I don't recall saying that to you, Ms. Reich. Others, maybe, at a private dinner last week ..."

The female guard pushed her left arm and the other gave a more forceful nudge. *This is getting old.*

In quick succession, everyone spoke but her.

"How did you know that I said that? You weren't there."

"Don't be cocky, missy," the female guard hissed.

"You're pretty foolish if you think you're just going to walk away from this, princess," the other said.

Pierce's jaw tensed and his eyes narrowed. A vein bulged on his temple. The phone ringing probably didn't help.

"Who is your contact in my network?"

Pierce, once again, stood right in front of her in another vain attempt to intimidate. He left the phone ringing and waited only a second before repeating the question.

"Who is your contact, Ms. Reich?"

An old classic film crossed her mind, and an all too familiar name popped into her head. She couldn't stop an emerging smirk. Her father, with a twinkle in his eye, used it at parties where people didn't know him.

"My contact's name?"

"Yes! The name!"

"You really want to know?"

"Now, Reich!"

"His name is Bond, James Bond. He's on Her Majesty's Secret Service, and I assure you that should anything happen to me, MI6 will be all over Pierce Industries." Without thinking, Reich went with her story, some truth, some not. "Your private life will be in shambles, your stocks will fall. You will be penniless as you watch helplessly all your ventures collapse. At any rate, I'm sure you know Mr. Bond's number. That could be him on the phone right now." Reich had difficulty suppressing her grin. She watched his eyes widen and hoped he would at least laugh or give her some credit for her presentation, but as the shock of her response wore off, it only seemed to anger him more.

Aw, come on! You gotta give me something for delivery. The man had no sense of humor. *Yet another flaw in the sack of shit's miserable character.*

"Do you think this a game, Ms. Reich? Do you know who I am?" he asked, his anger clearly mounting while the phone continued to ring.

Reich glanced at the underage girl and remembered her name, age and circumstances. Revulsion flared for a moment, but she tamed her anger and looked right into his eyes. She kept her voice low and deliberate. "I know who you are, Sir Pierce. You should get the phone. It's Mr. Robert Benson, your finance manager, calling from your New York office."

Reich enjoyed the confusion and nervousness on his face. He moved away from her towards the phone. *Yeah ... I know what you're thinking. "How does she know that? How could she know that?"* After so many other missions and other similar situations, all their looks of surprise looked the same.

"Hello," he said tentatively. The anxiety in his expression grew as he listened. Reich sighed and casually retrieved the small tablet she kept in the pocket under her belt.

The male guard stopped her with a firm grip on her elbow, and then extended his hand for the tablet.

"Are you sure you really want it?" Reich asked.

"Do you really want your front teeth?"

That was good. A quick response for the muscle.

"Go on," the female guard said.

"All right," Reich pretended to be reluctant and handed the tablet to the male guard. His grip would loosen very soon.

"There have been no arrests here, Robert! How can my investments crash when nothing has happened? I haven't been charged with anything ... For God's sake, Robert, I'm at my party, not under arrest ..."

Reich would've liked to hear more, but the guard released her tablet and hit the floor with a loud thud. Pierce dropped the phone from his ear and stared wide-eyed in disbelief that one of his guards lay flat on his back. As the female guard went to her fallen comrade's side, Reich casually moved away and consulted her tablet.

"Rachael? What's the meaning of this?"

"I don't know, sir. He was just touching her tablet and then this."

"Ah, Sir Pierce? In about ten seconds, Mr. Benson will hear from the United States Federal Trade Commission regarding a couple of federal indictments. And in about one minute, your private phone will ring. Your director of operations, Janice Phelps, will need to scrap your telecommunication satellite project tomorrow due to an electronic issue. It happened during the launch sequence ten minutes ago," Reich said.

Pierce frowned and shook his head. His attention shifted back to the phone. Reich put her tablet back in her belt and walked over to a pair of paintings—Renoirs—absolutely gorgeous.

"… The Federal Trade Commission said what!" Pierce yelled.

Undaunted, Reich moved to another set of paintings—two lesser known Van Goghs—perfectly illuminated.

"Beautiful. Excellent lighting can make a huge difference." The phone slammed into its cradle behind her. She turned. Pierce stood just inches away from her, held back by his own guard.

"You must have broken in here last week! You must have downloaded information from my computer! That's why we found nothing stolen! That's the only way you could know all these things! I'm going to—"

"You're going to what, Mr. Pierce? File charges on a crime that never happened?"

"I'll—I'll sue you—"

"Sue me for what? Not that it matters. In twenty minutes, your stock will be worth twenty cents on the dollar, at which point Reich Enterprises will buy up all the shares for controlling interests of Pierce Industries."

Pierce's eyes and veins bulged, enraged and stunned at the same time, and just beyond him, the young Antoinette looked very nervous. Pierce pulled away from the guard and walked to his desk. A phone rang in the adjacent room, and he slowed for a moment before glancing sharply back at her. Pierce remained still while he opened a drawer and pulled out a semi-automatic weapon.

"Sir Pierce, no! She's not worth it!" the female guard said.

"I don't know how you did all of this, Reich, but you will not live to enjoy your ill-gotten gains." Pierce pulled the trigger. It clicked but didn't fire. He checked the gun's safety catch, then pointed it right at her and pulled the trigger again. Another click.

"Well, this is interesting," Reich said, trying not to sigh in case he mistook her boredom for fear. "Usually the guy with the gun does a quick monologue about how he won and how it must suck to be at the other end of the gun. I have to say I do respect his quick action, not at all what I expected from a pig like you." She looked at her tiny wristwatch and wondered when the good guys would arrive.

"What the hell?"

"'Ill-gotten gains?' Who says that? I mean really? That sounds like something from one of the Bronte sisters ... Charlotte Bronte, actually. More of a Jane Eyre thing," Reich said.

Pierce kept pulling the trigger, but each time, it only clicked, and he glared down at the gun looking for something wrong. His lips pressed more tightly together, his jaw grew more rigid and his frown deepened with each futile attempt.

"The firing pin has been removed, Sir Pierce."

Pierce's eyes widened to a degree that Reich thought was humanly impossible. Before he could utter a word, the office doors burst off their hinges, and a group of tactical police and detectives rushed in.

Talk about timing. Okay, does everyone see this piece of filth has a gun on me?

Surrounded by the mass of authorities, Pierce dropped his weapon. Uniformed men and women seized everyone. Reich smiled as more shock and awe washed over Pierce's face.

"It's her! She stole data from my computer!" he shouted.

The police rounded up Reich as well as Pierce, the guard, Marie Antoinette, and the unconscious guard at her feet. She was pleased to see that two women and a man donned plastic gloves and moved almost reverently to the paintings she'd been looking at.

The agitation and confusion in Pierce's expression deepened as a detective approached him. "What is the meaning of this? Why are you here?"

"Detective Bradley at your service, my liege," a stout, older man, who clearly loved his processed food, said with a twinkle in his eye.

With his portly stature and disheveled appearance, Chief Inspector Arthur Bradley of Scotland Yard looked nothing like his official file picture. Reich had thought he might appear in the raid, even though her reconnaissance had put him in the United States twenty-four hours earlier—probably meeting with General Farrell. Reich was glad they'd prepared for alternate escapes.

"My name is Sir Robert Phillip Pierce—"

"Detective Bradley, these paintings are original Renoirs and Van Goghs," one of the women interrupted. "They are well preserved and this one is from the Isabella Stewart Gardner Museum—this is remarkable, sir."

Detective Bradley appeared to suppress a smile before turning back to Pierce. He took his time before he spoke, and timed each word with scratching his gray hair and flexing his fingers. "I guess getting you for receiving stolen national treasures isn't the human trafficking charges I had hoped to file, my liege, but it will do very nicely."

Reich smiled as she watched Pierce's expression move from anger to shock to fury within seconds.

"I don't own any real Van Goghs, Renoirs, or anything like that! I … I was set up! Someone broke in here last week—"

The jovial detective cut him off. "So, let me guess—instead of taking anything, which thieves are known to do, the bandits left you priceless paintings. Now that's a group of thieves that aren't straight on the purpose of grand theft! Yes, my liege—they left you priceless treasures rather than stealing them. Now that just makes perfect sense. Will that be your defense, my Worshipness?" Reich enjoyed Detective Bradley's sarcasm directed squarely at Pierce, but then the detective's gaze fell on the young Antoinette and his expression turned to worry and concern. He walked towards her.

"And how old are you, little one?" he asked in the tone a parent might use with a child. Reich remembered that Bradley had two granddaughters, eight and ten.

The girl didn't reply, and another officer, an older woman, stepped up beside her. "It's all right, dear. You won't get in trouble."

After a moment of unnatural silence, a small voice spoke. "I'm fourteen."

Bradley nodded, as it he'd expected that answer, and turned back to Pierce, clenching and unclenching his fists.

Reich suspected he was trying to control an impulse to hit Pierce. No one would blame him.

"I truly don't know which part of you I detest most, Pierce. Fortunately, I'm just a lowly public servant, and it will be up to the judge and God to decide your fate." Bradley looked away, clearly revolted by his proximity. He motioned his officers to take him away, then turned back to instruct the female officer. Pierce moved slowly, allowing the young lady to go first, then rushed Reich and slapped her with his unrestricted hand. The slap stung, but Reich went with the momentum and spun in place while bringing her leg into a roundhouse kick. It caught Pierce in the jaw. By the time the officer who'd been binding his hands caught up to him, Pierce lay on the ground out cold next to the unconscious guard.

Reich took a moment to feel her jaw while she looked over her handiwork. "Pig."

The detective stood over the fallen prisoner and smiled, seemingly unconcerned about Pierce's condition. Bradley nudged him with his foot to make sure he was unconscious and nodded approvingly. A devilish smile came over him as he looked up at Reich.

Reich wondered if he knew about the INTERPOL thing last month. She suspected that he did.

"And to top things off, I am in the presence of still further mysteries," Detective Bradley said.

"Me? I'm just another party guest, detective. I wish I was more than—"

"Just stop, Ms. Reich. I know who you are. And just off the record, I'd let you walk out for clobbering this punk, but that's not entirely my call. INTERPOL is on their way here to talk to you. While I appreciate your staff giving us the heads-up on the 'king,' and the artwork, I'm still a law enforcement officer, and in light of your history of slipping through our fingers, no matter how noble, I need to detain you. Once they're done, you and I need to have a serious chat about your prior work and adventures." He pulled a pair of handcuffs from his pocket and motioned for her to turn around.

Yup ... all the things they said about Chief Inspector Bradley's tenacity and determination are all true. Plan B.

"All right, Detective, but could I please go to the bathroom to check my mouth, relieve myself and please ... do you have some other bindings? I'm allergic to certain metals."

"Allergic? Really? You're allergic to handcuffs?"

"No, sir. I'm allergic to certain metals. Anaphylaxis. Not pretty once it gets started."

She stroked her face as if it still hurt, and coughed. Bradley stopped handcuffing her, looked her straight in the eyes, and considered the requests. He nodded to a larger woman to join him while he produced one of the plastic ties often used for mass arrests. Relieved, Reich took a good look at the woman. *Officer Virginia Spenser. Wrestler in college, national competitor, and just started a serious mix martial arts program. He's not taking any chances.*

"All right, Ms. Reich, but I want you to wear these, and Officer Spenser will join you in the closet while you take care of business. I'll be outside and close at hand, if you don't mind."

"Are you kidding? Do I look like I'm a threat?"

Bradley chuckled as he firmly tied her hands in front of her.

"With you? The Houdini of the FBI and INTERPOL interrogations rooms? No, I am not kidding. I take you very seriously, Ms. Reich. And I'm not going to miss an opportunity to talk to you later about much bigger things."

He tested the binds to make sure they held her wrists firmly, then took her arm and walked with her while Officer Spenser followed.

Thorough and not too trusting. Damn it! His record doesn't do him justice.

"You know there are several bathrooms on the ground floor," she suggested.

"And I'm sure they also have wonderful windows you could somehow slip through. In fact, why use windows? You've done that before. I think I'll find one that's three stories up with a thin skylight or no window at all, if you don't mind."

Bradley methodically opened and closed doors until he found a bathroom. Then he asked Spenser to watch her closely and disappeared into the bathroom. After a minute, he emerged with a small grin. "Well, Pierce does like his baths. Anyway, please do not attempt to go through the window—it's a sheer forty-foot drop."

Reich stood for just a moment giving the best annoyed look she could muster. Not deterred, Bradley gestured her in. "So, I have to keep these on? What happens if I need to .... you know?"

"You were going to have to wipe regardless. That's why Spenser's here."

"Really?" *Wow ... no chances with this guy. I bet Lux and Vespere would like him too. I bet he's hairy all over and he's the perfect height for them.*

"No problem, love. I've had to do this before."

Reich did her best to not chuckle at Spenser's pleasant response; her soft voice was somewhat incongruous with the thick-set, muscular woman.

"And don't be cheeky—Spenser here was quite the wrestler in her day," Bradley warned.

Reich marched into the bathroom with Spenser hot on her trail while the detective left the door ajar so he could listen. Reich walked straight to the toilet, extended both arms in front of her as far as she could, then retracted them quickly and forcefully into her chest. Her elbows jutted beyond her back, and the plastic binds broke, freeing her hands. Reich turned and threw a punch deep into Spenser's solar plexus. The officer gasped, the air knocked from her, and tried to keep from doubling over. Reich clamped one hand over Spenser's mouth and nose and wrapped both legs around the woman's waist. She struggled for air and tried to stay on her feet while Reich continued to apply pressure on the woman's torso and talked as if nothing were happening.

"You don't have to grimace. I didn't get a chance for a wax."

The woman's knees weakened and her eyes rolled upwards. Reich released her legs, stood, and guided the woman down so she didn't crash to the floor and bring the detective inside. Once the semi-conscious officer lay on the floor, Reich took a thread from her pocket and placed it, a micro-transponder and transceiver, on the woman's collar, then she moved to the bathroom vanity and flushed the toilet.

"All right, it's time for you to wipe." Reich hoped she said it with enough indignation. She dug deep into the back of the cabinet and was rewarded with the black satchel that contained climbing gear and lines.

"No. That was a courtesy flush," she said and flushed a second time.

Ironic ... Pierce being right about nothing being taken last week but leaving a whole lot of stuff behind ... the art was costly, though.

While the toilet filled with water, she unpacked the bag, hooked the rope to the toilet and tossed the other end out the small window. She slid into the climbing harness with well-practiced ease and was partially out the window when Spenser started to cough. Reich pushed off and rappelled down the four stories. She was releasing herself from the harness when Bradley yelled from forty feet above.

"Damn it! Reich! Stop right there! Just stop!"

Reich never looked back; she oriented herself and ran towards the closest ten foot wall by the road. She hoped Lux was waiting there as planned and not indulging herself with those damn chestnuts and lemons.

She sprinted through the manicured garden, dodging low branches and exposed roots, until she came to the estate's wall, a hundred feet from the main gate and road. Without slowing, she scaled a low-lying branch then a series of other branches and ended up a few feet from the wall.

She slid over the wall and hung there for a moment in preparation, then let go and dropped the remaining ten feet. She remained crouched until she saw Lux leaning against her car throwing chestnuts in the air and catching them in her waiting mouth.

"Lux! What the hell, woman! You'd think you might be a bit more discreet and wait in the car? What if security found you ..." Reich stopped as her field of vision around the car widened to include a pile of three estate guards lying unconscious on the ground.

"Hmm. Show-off."

"This Sir Pierce person should hire more qualified guards. They got in their own way when they tried to take me. Not bad for a small one like me," Lux said as she bit into another chestnut.

"I don't know how small you're going to be if you keep eating those things. They're not without calories." Reich didn't wait for a response. She slipped into the back seat of the car before Lux could see her smile.

Lux slid behind the wheel and turned on the ignition. "Oh ... the giant loses all her fat, gains some muscles, lets her hair grow, and suddenly she's a lethal weapon with an opinion on weight. How things have changed."

Reich smiled. Things certainly had changed since she'd met Lux at Thanksgiving. She wondered how Anthony was doing, and figured he'd be surprised at how she looked now.

Her smile broadened as she settled back into the fine leather upholstery and picked up one of four waiting tablets. The luxury sedan pulled out, and before she could ask for confirmation of the other missions, a text came through on her main tablet. "It looks like Vespere and Bella successfully hindered Pierce's telecommunication satellite launch."

Lux nodded as she expertly drove the high-end car and popped yet another chestnut into her mouth. "Yes, oh Great One. Further, Pax has our gear, residence, and visas ready for our trip back to the United States. Fitting, I should say, but still," she looked back at Reich through the rear-view mirror, "your insistence on handling these missions yourself, as well as these ancillary ones, is dangerous."

Reich sighed. She'd been about to argue, but Lux was right. "I know. We have eight years to prepare the world for the shock of discovering an advanced, new world hiding behind the sun's corona, and less than four years before the Earth's atmosphere is irreversibly affected by methane build-up. It's just that ... well, it's just that ..."

"It's just that if we have a chance to save a few souls along the way, like those children in Moscow, the village in Brazil, the slaves in Hong Kong, the prostitutes in Berlin and the underage young woman back there, we should, right? Yes ... just like Perez ... I hate to admit it, but he chose his successor wisely," Lux said.

The corners of Reich's mouth pulled up at the reluctant compliment. "That had to hurt."

"Yes. Yes, it did."

Reich looked back at her series of tablets and refocused on her master plan.

"Once we have control of the stocks and assets of Pierce's empire, we'll be able to refit his satellite with ours so we can have a direct, clear link with Terra. Maybe they have some ideas on this methane poisoning thing. The sooner we deal with that, the better chance we have of handling the culture shock of their existence."

Lux looked at her again and nodded in agreement. "Have faith, Reich. Between all of us, we'll be able to save the Earth and keep it from falling apart regarding our existence. You handled it pretty well and you were put under great stress. And with your knowledge regarding the United States government, you will be the best person for the task of convincing them to trust us."

"True, but I am one person. For those who believe we're alone, and discover that we've never been alone, it will be a major shock of identity and core beliefs ... Perez was right, there are bigger things to deal with," Reich said as she looked through the darkened window.

"Very true."

Reich's tablet blinked and issued a quiet buzzing noise followed by the familiar female voice. "Attention—a recent recording has just been downloaded. I focused on three individuals only: Chief Inspector Arthur Bradley, Officer Virginia 'Ginny' Spenser and Officer John 'Jack' Middleton. The audio and transcript has been filtered and compiled five point three minutes ago, real time. Icons and last names will appear beside their text and audio statements. Are you prepared?"

"Yes. Please initiate, and put their full personal and professional files on the green tablet for review. Transmit audio to the front of the car for Lux to hear as well. Begin."

> *Spenser: " ... Owen! Ramsey! Stop screwing around and lock that evidence down! INTERPOL is almost here and the boss is pretty pissed! Don't .... too many times ..."*

Bradley: "... Will someone explain to me how one woman got her hands on rappelling equipment, cleared a forty foot drop, ran, unobserved no less, across half an acre of lawn, scaled a ten plus foot wall, took out one of my officers and three of Pierce's private security, and drove away in a waiting car? It's pretty embarrassing when Scotland Yard and London's finest can't contain one woman, even if she is the famous Christine Reich. Anyone care to explain? I hate feeling like the only idiot."

Spenser: "I wouldn't be too hard on yourself, sir. The woman was like a cat with as many lives, I tell you. By the time I turned around she already knocked the hell out of me. She took me down in under twenty seconds."

Middleton: "And she did the same thing in an INTERPOL security station, an interrogation room with the usual high-tech surveillance system and no windows."

Reich picked up the green tablet, flipped to Middleton's file and looked at his icon again so she could picture the three of them together. Compared to Bradley and Spenser, he was taller, thinner and impeccably dressed. His bio indicated he was a literature major at University of Cambridge.

Middleton: "I must say that Sir Pierce may have a point about someone breaking in and leaving stuff. I mean, Reich didn't have the rappelling equipment on her person, and I'm sure Pierce wouldn't keep that kind of equipment in the bathroom..."

Spenser: "That sexual deviant would, I bet."

Middleton: "While that may be true, I think Reich put everything in place, including her escape route. She set Sir Pierce up with the artwork, informed us and did her usual disappearing act. I think I already know the answer to this, but I wouldn't be doing my job if I didn't ask."

Bradley: "Out with it, Jack. I get short-tempered when I'm prickly. Escaped material witnesses and mysteries don't sit well with me."

Middleton: "Should we investigate Pierce's allegation of being set up in light of Reich's escape, or just let his legal team fight that one as he rots in a dungeon?"

Bradley: "Are you kidding me? Is that a trick question?"

Spenser: "That slick piece of crap will somehow dodge the child trafficking and sexual assault charges like he always does, but he'll hang on the stolen art. Sounds like a great example of justice and irony going hand in hand, if you ask me."

Middleton: "That's pretty philosophical for a former wrestler. Oh, but maybe you're changing approaches to things now? You know, going for brains rather than brawn since catwoman took you out back there."

Spenser: "Hey, Middleton! I thought keeping the perimeter secured was under your watch, college boy? Nice job, you sack of ..."

Bradley: "Enough, you two! We've got to focus on this Reich woman. She does right by putting the bad guys in the shitter, but I want to know what's it all about. I mean, she got her hands on some stolen art, put it in that pig's castle, and just walked away, setting him up on a charge that will actually stick. She did this out of the kindness of her heart? For nothing? And her other little jaunts around the world doing the same thing are just for kicks?"

Spenser: "That stunt she did in Moscow was pretty over the top. Kind of like Perez back in the day. Dangerous, but in a good way. He fell off the planet, too."

Bradley: "Hong Kong three months ago ... Yeah ... and I want to talk to her before she does too. I'm positive there's something bigger than acts of kindness motivating Reich and her resources ..."

Middleton: "'I'll chase him round Good Hope, and round the Horn, and round the Norway Maelstrom, and round perdition's flames before I give him up.' Herman Melville, sir. The American novelist who wrote Moby Dick. Looks like we're after the great white whale, sir. It seems particularly apt here."

Spenser: "Smart ass."

Bradley: "All right, Macbeth, get General Farrell on the line. Tell him we got a sighting and actually had Reich in custody, but she did another Houdini ... guess ... heading out of country and, based on her track record, to the US."

Spenser: "And let the games and quotes begin."

Bradley: "Yes. Let them quotes begin ... 'To the last, I grapple with thee.'"

"End of recording. Will archive in recent storage for further analysis," her tablet said.

"Please continue monitoring and notify me as close to real time as possible."

"Acknowledged."

"Lux? Are we getting messy and predictable?"

"No, Reich. This Bradley and Farrell have been looking for us for several years. By the sound of that discussion, they have been working together as a team for years. They're good, very good. New plan?"

Reich looked at her reflection in the window. "Yup. Berlin."

"Sounds like a plan." Lux popped a chestnut into her mouth.

"Bigger things to deal with and bigger challenges along the way. Just great."

Chapter Ten

**Arcadia Planitia, Mars, two miles under the Martian crust
… present day …**

IT WAS SO QUIET. *I do miss the other voices*, Master Architect Janus thought as he slowly opened his eyes from his nap. After all his time asleep, you would think he'd no longer be tired or want to sleep, but that wasn't the case.

He moved his limbs slowly, appreciative that the Keeper, the master computer, had revived other citizen survivors before him. The warmth of the blanket and bed was nothing compared to the encapsulating state of his Martian-made embryonic cryogenic stasis. The buoyancy of its warm, protein-enriched plasma had been unlike anything he had experienced before. The constant programming for keeping his intellect engaged when he was in cryogenic sleep was something he had thought might work but never had time to test.

The amazing computer had created an embryonic state programmed with literature, languages, science and mathematics, transmitted through a plasma medium to keep the mind active. It had felt as if he were talking or studying. *Impressive.*

Even so, he was still shocked by the knowledge that he was the seventy-eighth reincarnation of his former self, perfectly reproduced from his own stem cells so as to survive millions upon millions of full solar rotations.

Memories, new knowledge attainment via artificial intelligence, external processing; immortality while unconscious? Costly but fascinating. Little mystery as to why she wanted my DNA sample.

The last to be revived of a once great civilization, he was one of seventy-two fellow Martian survivors out of thirteen thousand who stayed behind while the others had left a doomed solar system.

Ironic. Those who left are probably long deceased.

Generations had passed, and he wondered how they'd evolved. Did they find the Originators? Would they recognize him and the others? They would be a great archaeological find, maybe even a missing link into whatever they have changed into. He guessed they might find out, someday. Perhaps.

"Am I disturbing you?" the Keeper said. Her voice was a lower baritone than he remembered, and more feminine. He assumed it was more likely a result of her own evolution, software modifications and the absences of other subroutine computer voices. His eyes still closed, Master Janus carefully formed words as he continued to slowly move his limbs and take deep, refreshing breaths.

"No, not at all. My original awakening was disturbing enough. Now? Nothing will ever compare to that awakening."

"Yes. That is accurate. I have been able to obtain the subtleties of irony and aspects of humor. I also have acquired the inability to avoid such obvious questions. The prior citizens did assist me over the great period of silence."

Janus was truly impressed with the computer's profound intellectual growth, personality development and explosion in sapience. Her personality, moral development and decision making processing were extraordinary. Nonetheless, her need to awaken many of his fellow citizens for company disturbed him. He understood that, like all life, she had chosen a path for her own survival.

Such a long period of isolation would have destroyed any life form. And her decision to sacrifice the few citizens, the sixty-three hundred, for her own survival while continuing the mission of survival indicated higher level sapience. Janus thought he would have made a similar decision.

"Are you disappointed by my means of continuing the mission, that I sacrificed others to preserve myself and the remaining survivors?"

Impressive. Artificially developed theory of mind. Very impressive.

"No. I cognitively understand it. I am still not used to your development and how you have become similar to us biological lifeforms. It will take me time to acclimate to this new development. It is not disappointment: it is surprise, amazement and intellectual curiosity in how you evolved, how similar you are to us, to me," Janus said as the thoughts popped into his head.

He took a deep breath to clear his thoughts and shifted focus from the computer's growth to the profound changes in his universe. Janus opened his eyes. Dim light illuminated his room. He rolled onto his side, curled up his legs, and asked his next set of questions.

"Based on our last briefings, please summarize the critical changes that require your awakening all of us all at once. If possible, keep the points under eight."

"Thank you for clarifying those parameters as there are one point three million key points I could make. I will need just a moment to isolate those points. Please hold."

Janus was surprised at how tiny his bedroom was, but it still contained a chair and a small table. A neatly folded pile of clothes sat on it next to a pitcher and two cups.

Who is the chair for if I am here?

"Master Janus? Specific points summary completed. Just so you are aware and not surprised, Citizen Olympia will be here to assist you shortly. Are you ready?"

"Yes." It took him a moment to remember that Olympia was the older female as opposed to Athena, the younger one.

"Points are arranged from lower to higher priority: Venus experienced a runaway greenhouse effect, resulting in the need to abandon the planet; the surface of our home world was devastated by impact craters and changes in our planetary axis from the destruction of Gemini Alpha and Beta planets; Architect Iris relocated the hominem species from Venus to Terra; this species adapted more readily to the environment than the species already there. To date, the original Terrans are extinct, along with their ancestors on Earth. In regards to Earth, the impact craters destroyed the various dinosaur species; the impact also altered its axis as well but to a more favorable outcome, allowing for the mammal species to develop; the Earth's Keeper is eight percent operational which resulted in the Earther hominems to develop without support."

"Hold," Janus said. "They developed without guidance? No master computer to assist their development. Was this one of the experiments carried out by Architect Hades?"

"No, it was not Architect Hades's experiment. Yes, the hominems did develop without a Keeper."

"And Hades made Terra work?"

"Yes. More surprisingly, the Terran project transformed the planet into a small civilization of one point nine billion hominems. By changing terraform equipment into breathable atmosphere and heating generators, he forfeited the atmosphere and surface area for an underground civilization along the terminal line. Further, he combined its power with solar energy to power an array of holographic emitters that has rendered the planet invisible to hominems' visual wavelength, making the planet invisible. Its machinery, however, is failing after being in operation non-stop since Earth's space age. Unfortunately, Terra's orbit, which kept the sun between itself and Earth, has been altered, and Terra will imminently be in line of sight to the Earth for the first time in its existence."

Young, impetuous, impulsive and brilliant. Hades had seen things that others could not. "I am impressed with Architect Hades's abilities. He proves once again that it is adaptation, not intelligence, that is key to survival. His tidal-locked planet not only survived all this time but has maintained its own records and ours. I am sure that Terra's Keeper assisted in keeping you updated?"

"Yes, whenever we were in orbital proximity. I must say as a way of conveying my appreciation for the Terran Keeper, that her communications were key to my survival. It has been too long since our last communication."

Yes ... she has become emotional, he thought. "And Architect Iris? What happened to her?"

"Sadly, she perished on Venus. She refused to leave her Venusian Keeper. I lost contact with both of them."

Janus knew that both of the architects were long gone. Still, hearing that Iris died with her keeper saddened him. "I am sorry."

"Yes. I was too," the computer said.

Sad and sorry? Quite the development. "Are there more points?"

"Here are the key points: Terran's efforts to propagate the hominem species via cross breeding has been partially effective, but they remain as an endangered species. Once the Terran's orbital pattern clears the sun and its cloaking technology fails, Earth hominem species will know of their existence. They have had the technology to see Terra without its cloak for fifty-one of its years. Both Terran and Earther Keepers have been partially effective in keeping Terran's existence obfuscated on Earth. Their success is now dwindling. Both Keepers, as well as myself, are concerned with the Earthers' existential response to possessing direct confirmation that they are not alone in their own solar system. The Earthers are primitive due to their wild curiosity with no guidance from their Keeper."

"What a fascinating experiment. A hominem species allowed to form its own civilizations, its own concepts, without the assistance of a master computer or an architect. Their ideas of who they are and their point of view of the universe must be extraordinary. They must have thought they were gods in the absence of other similar species. You will have to tell me more of this later. Please go on," Janus said. It took him a moment to rein in his scientific curiosity.

"Yes. They are a different species—technologically moving at a slow but steady pace while their view of their place in the universe is that of an infant. I will elaborate later. The Earthers are slowly coming to terms with the fact that their planet's exosphere and biosphere are in danger. With the efforts of Terran recruits from Earth's own population, there is movement in identifying the methane crisis and possible containment. Still, on a profound scale, we have identified the source of the oxygen/hydrogen beam bombardment of the Jovian planet, Jupiter, as coming from far outside our galaxy. The technology to deliver such an astronomical quantity of oxygen and hydrogen consistently remains a near incalculable mystery that we are attempting to determine," she said gravely.

Though he said nothing, Janus immediately concluded the net result of such an act, a leap of creativity versus logic and reason. "Based on your calculations, how long will it take for the oxygen and the additional hydrogen to ignite Jupiter's atmosphere?"

The dialogue had been so steady that the sudden silence while the Keeper calculated seemed very long.

"Speculation would place the probability of Jupiter becoming a viable second sun between one and three full solar cycles. In order for it to ignite, there will need to be an actual trigger. While the source of these beams is outside our galaxy, there will need to be a massive spark, an explosion of a solar-sun level to ignite Jupiter even if the oxygen and hydrogen levels reached threshold level or beyond. This is unusual. How did you speculate that Jupiter would ignite?"

"A wild guess. Now here's another question: have you run the entire light radiation spectrum on Jupiter since we last spoke, before I went into cryonics sleep?"

Before he'd been forced to his cryogenic stasis, he'd witnessed Jupiter's x-ray and gamma radiation levels following the Gemini collisions. At the time, he'd thought it was an abnormal effect of such a blast. *But with the presence of such light elements?*

More silence followed, longer this time as the keeper collected, collated and analyzed calculations and measurements at amazing speed. But as brilliant as the master computer was, the difference between Janus and his Keeper, for now, was imagination and the classic 'what if.'

"I … I have missed you greatly, Master Architect Janus. I continue to be amazed at your species' ability to stretch their mind beyond reason. There are subatomic particles emitting radiation well beyond x-ray levels at Jupiter's center. Should the oxygen-hydrogen levels continue to increase, the subatomic particle's density will expand to the level of a subatomic black hole, enough mass to ignite the planet. Have you already guessed what will happen to the planets?"

I don't even want to think about it.

"No." He opened his eyes and smiled even as thoughts of doom and destruction from a series of catastrophic events flooded his mind. "What direction do these oxygen-hydrogen beams come from? From where do they originate? Are they from the last known heading of our people, to the Originators?"

"Yes, Master Architect Janus. The heading follows the course of our ancestors. It follows the path to the Originators. What does it mean?"

A path to the gods? The Master Originators—the ones who with their mere thoughts and words made the heavens, planets, life and us. Were we all part of the plan? Are they to me as I am to Terran's rattus? Janus thought, finding no words to articulate his thoughts.

"I don't know, but it's just like last time ... Gemini Alpha and Beta 'just fell out of their orbits' as if simply pushed, completely altering our solar system. And now the mysterious appearance of the right amount of chemical gas elements and a subatomic black hole come together to ignite a gas giant into a small, unstable star ... Mysteries or messages from the Originators? I don't know. But it may be time to find out. And we may need our Terran and Earther cousins to assist," Janus said as he carefully sat up and swung his feet over the side of the bed in one smooth move. He was glad to see he was all in one piece and in control of his limbs, torso and faculties. "And it may be time for us to meet our descendants or even maybe the Originators. How great would that be?"

"Just to reiterate, I did miss you. Your ability to change a cataclysmic event on a galactic scale into an opportunity to meet our future, our gods, is ... amazing."

Our gods? She sees herself as part of their creation? Truly fascinating.

"Yes ... I am very good at that." His bedroom door opened. A dim light spilled in from the corridor, creating a silhouette of a female in the doorway. Olympia.

This could be interesting, he thought as he stepped out of his bed, feeling pressure on his feet for the first time in millions of annual cycles.

Chapter Eleven

Time, space, plane of existence … unknown...

"WHY DO YOU CONTINUE to focus on this speck of the universe when there is so much more to explore?" one of many voices asked in a sea of different voices and simultaneous thoughts.

"Because they are the genesis of those that traveled far to find us. They are part of our corporeal past. They are the past. Doesn't that pique your curiosity?" the voice said.

"Yes," one voice said above the many. "But then everything piques our curiosity, no matter how small."

"Then why did you ask?"

"Perchance there might be another answer I did not anticipate. Why are you changing their solar system again?"

"They are an interesting species, corporeal with limited life expectancy, but they evolve rapidly, especially when confronted with obstacles. They remind me of our earlier times when we were required to adapt, a shadow of our former selves when time was linear. They give me reason to explore. They inspire me to find our creator. Do you remember?"

The voices fell silent as curiosity and focus shifted to the species located in a minute speck of the universe.

"Shall we observe together?" a sole voice asked.

"Yes. We will observe," the voices said in unison, declaring their will to be in one place at one time to watch how the species would respond to the new events.

"What will they do?" one of many voices asked. This genuine question absent an answer was an unusual experience. Even speculation of what might come next was difficult.

"I do not know," the sole voice said. "We shall see."

Excitement rippled through the voices. Another unusual experience not felt in nearly thirty-seven million years.

About the Author

In addition to creating the *Birds of Flight* series and the other award-winning science fiction stories, *Future Prometheus* and *Intelligent Design*, Erickson holds a BA in psychology and sociology from Boston College and a master's degree in psychiatric social work from the Simmons School of Social Work. Certified in cognitive behavioral treatment and a post-trauma specialist, he is also a senior instructor of psychology and counseling at Cambridge College, visiting lecturer at Salem State University's School of Social Work and a senior therapist in a clinical group practice in the Merrimack Valley, Massachusetts. To learn more about the author, his writing and future projects, please look at the following websites:

Blog - www.jmeindieblog.com
Author's website – www.jmericksonindiewriter.com
Publisher's website - www.jmericksonindiewriter.net